bElonG

BELONG

FAZLE HASNAYEN

Srishti
PUBLISHERS & DISTRIBUTORS

Srishti Publishers & Distributors
N-16, C. R. Park
New Delhi 110 019
srishtipublishers@gmail.com

First published in Canada, 2006

This edition published by
Srishti Publishers & Distributors in 2007
Second impression 2012

Typeset in AGaramond 11pt. by Suresh Kumar at Srishti

Printed and bound in India

This edition is only for sale in Indian sub-continent.

This book is dedicated
to Nilofar – my love,
and my family.

Acknowledgement

Heartfelt thanks to Misty for the concept of cover and the sketch, Brij Kishore for putting down the concept on canvas, which I scanned and made it a component of cover page. In addition, my friends like Ashok and Ashi who always kept on insisting me to finish this story, and everyone who had encouraged me to go ahead with this idea. I thank Trafford Publishing to have given me a forum to present this book to you. And above all, to you, for holding the book in your hands and encouraging me to write more.

Foreword

'Belong is the story of Divaker – a common and ordinary man like one of us. 'Belong' is the tale of ordinary human life with all its problems and challenges, as seen and experienced through the eyes and life of Divaker.

He is one of us, an average human being. He belongs to a 'lower-middle income' family of a remote village in West Bengal, but the family kept on moving from place to place ever since Divaker was a child with all the utensils, table-fan, mattress and radio.

Papa was an average government servant. As a child, Divaker had seen people moving away before becoming friend, people who never came back ever. Before he could mix-up with local kids at school, it was time for Divaker to move off to a new place.

Divaker saw a lot of turbulence in his teen years. Maa and Papa separated, and he was sent to a Hindu boy's missionary school up in the hills, where life started everyday at five-thirty in the morning, all twelve months of the year. He had jumped into manhood by the time he passed high school. He somewhere missed the inquisitiveness and curiosity of teen age and the heavenly-dreamy period of youth. He was a full-grown man at twenty, a man with invisible wrinkles on face.

Divaker crawled, stood on his feet, walked and ran for career, life and money. He tasted varied flavors of success, failures and disgust. He carved out a small position for himself in this big-biiiiig world. Life taught him the way this world goes round the sun – harder way round.

Divaker married, after a full-time romance of four years, it was then he discovered and learnt few other things in life, not all of them pleasant – yes, the harder way round.

Contents

1

The Train to Lucknow

It rained pretty fine last night. The type of rain you generally do not see in late December. Raindrops still holding it to leaves and rolling down gradually, then falling on the grass, then gradually, slowly seeping down into already saturated mud. It is late December, yes, the whole year gone by. Many such years have gone by, just as if the water drops falling now from the leaves. Then, those years unknowingly find its way to the already saturated sphere of memory. It is early in the morning now.

He sat by the window, listening to the sound of a new day waking up, from the coziness of the dark and wet night. Time flew by, at a pace where turning back is unthinkable, unimaginable, especially the last ten years, no maybe fifteen, no maybe twenty. Whatever, time really flew away fast for him, or maybe for everyone. He turned away from the window to face the darkness of his room – which was not as bright as outside.

What next? Lot of things. Toilet, brushing, shaving, bath, tea, breakfast, ironing, shoes, etc… etc… etc. The train for Lucknow leaves at seven thirty. It's already around six.

He checked the tickets again as he boarded the train and soon found his small share of space that he bought for the seven hours and five hundred kilometers – seat number thirty nine. Thirty nine is a multiple of thirteen, his lucky number. He was born on this date. Maa and Papa always used to say that it was a lucky number for them. They 'got' him on this date. They used to relate a lot of things to the lucky number. Even the sum of their old motorcycle registration number turned out thirteen. He didn't know exactly from when, but he tried to find a relation between any numeric things to his lucky number. Habits don't die fast. They maybe good, bad or useless as this one, but they linger on, like something from the past. Unavoidable and unpurposeful. He sat by the window looking at the platform, People, faces, and noises, all mixed up, creating a single thing. He is also a part of this single thing.

He is Divaker Acharya – a part of this single thing.

The train pulled, first by inches, then by meters. Slowly and smoothly, it pulled more and more, pulling him away from the single thing – the people, faces and noises. The single thing then became a lot of things – buildings, roads, cars, drains, and slums-changing every moment, every mile, like an acrobat doing his job. Then it changed into rivers bridges, farms and villages. He was out of Delhi, but the stench of that single thing was somewhere, then everywhere. Perhaps he was carrying the stench. The stench of life, time and existence. Something one has to carry. Is this same for everyone? Or maybe everyone has a different stench. Something very personal and non-identical, like fingerprints. The continuous rhythm of iron wheels beating over rail track joints was gaining higher pitch every time.

A highway also runs close to the railroad. Cars, buses and trucks are all being left behind. He was on the same highway once, around ten years back. Destination was same. He was riding a new twelve horse power motorcycle; which he bought that time. New job, new bike, new cell phone and everything new. Was he carrying the stench that time? No, maybe not. Had it been there, he could have recalled it now. Heaven knows from where he picked up this nasty stench.

Anyway, it's not a problem these days. He often forgets all about it, just like stinking socks – the odour turns up only when you open up your shoelaces. Whenever he thinks of those days, he feels as if they were things of a previous life. A life that he lived, ended, and is reborn again to live this another life. Or is it the same life but the person has changed. The previous person has now been transformed into another person with a different set of brain receptors. That maybe the reason why he is not able to feel and perceive things, the way he used to earlier; or maybe because, he was getting old. The other day, they said on a National Geographic programme that people are getting old faster these days. He has just crossed thirty, somewhere in between the second and third multiple of thirteen. Five years of romance followed by four years of marriage.

The year when things started, he paid total of a hundred thousand rupees towards his mobile bills for the year. Things were quite different. He never knew she is the person he will fall in love, have a full-fledged love life, and a successful marriage. They just got together, and it just started. He was in Allahabad, winter of 1995 to attend marriage of Arif – his colleague. Arif and Divaker were both posted in Meerut- a mediocre town of western U.P – a place known for bed sheet and towel mills, communal riots and not known for its extreme climate and dust, lot of it everywhere. There in Allahabad, Divaker knew nobody except Arif and his family; mother and father, both old. Although he had spent a few years of his childhood in Allahabad, no not years, but months, two months of vacation every year for four years, adds up to few months.

Devyani and her family – father, mother and two sisters were their next-door neighbor. She was younger to Divaker by four years. Divaker's sister and Devyani were friends and Devyani used to come to their place very often. They were kids, played with dolls; often she had her lunch and dinner with them. He was a bigger kid, stepping in to teens. He paid no significant interest in their girlish business. He found older and grown up girls more fascinating. What did he know that this girl playing with his sister would one day become his wife.

He asked Arif to excuse him for an hour from the wedding ceremonies, and Arif agreed. He had made up his mind to find out what happened to that girl and her family. Were they still living in the same place? How far things have changed? He took a scooter from Arif and started for Mumfordgunj – this was the place they once lived. The place had changed a lot. It looked smaller now, with more people, shops and houses. Divaker could not recognize the two-room house his family once lived in. He had to make out- Yes, this is it!

Next house in the row was the one in which she lived. That had not changed a bit. A man of mid forties came out, half asleep, irritated for being disturbed off his afternoon nap. Divaker enquired for Mr. B. K. Mishra – Devyani's father – and the man informed that they left two years back. Mishra Uncle was in a government job. He was transferred two years back to Lucknow, so the family also shifted over. Later the man asked a boy wearing shorts to give a phone number and went inside without saying anything. Divaker held a piece of paper, her phone number written on it. Little did he know that those six digits were his password to an unknown future. Things that would just keep on happening and happening and happening and suddenly, he would know that the 'password' has given him access to his own life, half of which is already lived. Games destiny play – amazing!!!

Arif was waiting for him. Not him, perhaps, it's the scooter. Rest of the day just went by. In evening, the Baraat started for Lucknow. Five hours drive from Allahabad. Divaker was in a car with Arif and two other important people, important to Arif. All the way, he thought that he wouldn't call up Mishra Uncle's phone number. Just in case they invite him to their place, he will not be able to go. Often curiosity loses its charm once you know the answer. The mind loves to keep few things lingering on, enjoying it and avoiding to reach its end, like an orgasm. Yes, he would rather call, once he is back to Meerut. In case of latter, he can always give a false assurance to pay them a visit if he ever came to Lucknow.

The Baraat reached Lucknow a couple of hours before midnight. The marriage hall smelled sickly of marigold and stale roses. Rests of people were getting down from the bus that followed them from Allahabad. There were arrangements for them to freshen up and change clothes. Changing clothes means wearing a suit or a blazer and tie. The marriage hall was brightly lit with colorful lights, red, green, yellow, and blue, flashing and dancing cheaply. A loudspeaker blared numbers from movies at an outrageous volume. The 'Baraatis' were soon seen filling the space wearing all types of suits and ties, some ill fitting, others in odd colors. The dancing lights stubbornly reflected in everyone's sleepy eyes. The whole place smelled of food, matar paneer, dal makhani, aloo chaat, kadhi pakoda, fried rice, missi roti etc... etc..., all mixed up. He moved away from the place, feeling nausea and desperately in need of fresh air. As he walked to a distance where noise of the marriage hall fainted and was no longer irritating, he saw a telephone booth at the next corner. He fumbled the piece of paper in his pocket, it was there and the booth was open.

'Hello, whom do you want to talk?' a lady in her fifties asked in a low voice. This was Aunty. Devyani's mother.

'Hello, I'm Divaker.'

'Who Divaker?' a moments silence, 'Oh! Are you Padma's son?'

'Yes Aunty, it's me.'

Before he could realize, he gave commitment to visit them next morning.

Although Divaker had to start back for Meerut next morning, he did not. As he woke up he recalled the address Aunty told him last night over phone. It was 10 AM. Arif and his wedding kept him waking until the wee hours of the morning. He felt a mild headache and drowsiness. He took a quick bath, in a dark bathroom of the marriage hall. After taking leave from Arif, he hired a cab, and in forty-five minutes, he was in front of Mishra Uncle's house. Aunty opened the door. Her age now prominently reflected on her face and physique. She had also put on weight. She saw him from the window and opened the door in such haste that she almost stumbled upon something.

'You have grown up a lot,' she said, recognizing Divaker.

'Yeah.'

'You were a kid when I last saw you, never thought I can ever meet you people, when your Papa was transferred to Assam. I lost all hope. It's such a pleasant thing to see you again. How is Padma?' she smiled.

'Maa is ok, Fine. She always talks a lot about you, and says that she never had a friend like you.'

'I know, I know. Now you have come, I will have a chance to meet her again, I know that,' she said and smiled.

She also knew all the scandalous stuff that happened shortly before Divaker and the family left Allahabad, when Papa somehow managed to get a long distance transfer. Divaker made himself comfortable on the sofa, as Aunty went inside to bring water for him. She talked to him a lot about the days when both the families were neighbors. She was as happy as a kid, who has just found out a lost piece of toy. Her happiness was genuine and unselfish. She was really pleased to see him, and Divaker could make it out from her eyes and attitude.

From one of the rooms Devyani came to meet, next came her two other sisters – one older, other younger. Devyani had grown only in height, otherwise her face; smile, hair and everything else, were just the way as it was before. They all had a formal family sort of conversation. Everyone asked about everyone in the family, Papa, Maa and his sister Misty. Divaker had lunch with them and made a quick departure from their place, assuring to visit them, whenever he has a chance to come Lucknow. He hired an auto-riksha and got back to the railway station.

It was late afternoon and he was waiting at Lucknow railway station, for the train, which will take him back to Meerut in seven hours. He was feeling sleepy and his head felt heavy over shoulders, with loads of stuff running inside it. In half an hour, the train arrived. He placed the bag inside the seat, and as soon as he settled down, he was fast asleep. All this had happened ten years back.....

His present day journey was about to end. Journeys had always been an inseparable part of his life. So many journeys, that often he found it difficult to differentiate one from the other. The train had just loosened from Kanpur. In a little more than an hour, he will be in Lucknow. There was a time when his heartbeat increased as every kilometer of distance to Lucknow decreased. He does not feel it now. For the first time today, he turned back to see people inside the railway compartment. Why are people in all the journeys so similar? Some purpose or the other takes people here and there.

They all will get down and proceed to whatever reasons they have traveled all the way. He is also here for a reason. He is here to meet his wife, Devyani. She does not stay with him in Delhi. She is with her parents here in Lucknow. Slowly the train crawled into out-skirts of Lucknow. Again buildings, cars, shops, slums, bridges etc… etc… He could again smell the 'single thing' lurking somewhere near him. It is like a monster-playing hide and seek, enjoying every bit of the game. Every time he hides like a child, the monster finds him, slowly removes the curtain behind which he hides, and gives a malicious smile and says,

'See! I have got you again.'

Outer signal cabin of Lucknow station just passed. Minutes later the train was entering platform, slowly, panting and heaving like a tired serpent. The train stopped and people rushed out of it, and then joined a pre-existing crowd of people going to the platform exit. The whole thing looked like a flowing drain. Small drain joined bigger one, carrying garbage and polythene bags of all colors. He also joined it, and soon, he was dragged off automatically out of the station.

Outside, it is a different world. Rikshawallah, auto-drivers, cab drivers all hawked in to grab passengers, all of them.

'Saheb, give whatever you want, I will take you to a good hotel. Good rooms, color TV and hot water, only for three hundred rupees per day.' A rikshawallah pitched in.

He looked in the eyes of a cab driver and he perhaps understood what Divaker meant. He came near, and helped Divaker with the bag.

'Where to Sir?' the cab driver asked.

'Gomti Nagar,' Divaker said, and asked, 'how much?'

'Hundred rupees, Sir.'

'Fine.'

Practically this city has not changed much for the last ten years, except for a few shopping malls, where people go and click photograph of friends and family on escalators. Only population and encroachment has gone up, narrowing down the streets to half their width. The sights and sound of this city is very familiar to him. Burlington crossing, Vidhan sabha, Hazratganj, Nishatganj and lot other places passed by.

Really, the bigger things never change. The smaller things do. A kebabwallah, who used to vend at the corner of Nishatgunj Bridge is not there today. He used to eat kebab at his shop, sitting on his bike, every time on his way back from Devyani's home. It's a cloudy winter afternoon and the sky is overcast. It may rain and the mercury will further go down. The chilling winds of northern India simply touch the bones. It's already so cold here.

'It rained here yesterday, Sir,' the cab driver voluntarily added, reading his thoughts. In half an hour, he stood in front of her house. He paid the cab driver and pressed the doorbell.

She was smiling, as she opened the door, the same innocent smile. Really, it has not changed since the first time he saw her. It was not exactly the beauty of her smile, but the innocence, charm, simplicity and honesty that made it so very attractive. Broad lips and fluffy cheeks.

'How are you?' he plucked her cheeks.

'Hmmm.... Just as usual, how was your journey?'

'As usual, like most of the times.'

'Come, sit by the heater son,' Aunty meanwhile emerged from the room inside. He eased himself on the sofa. It was cozy indoors. Outside, the weather was inclement. Some time later he heard a thunder and then almost at the same time, it started to rain. He could hear the raindrops adamantly smashing on the streets, on the mosaic pavement of their house, near the gate and everywhere else. Devyani brought him a cup of tea. He sipped it and felt the warmth touch inside his body. It was soothing. He always praised Devyani for the fine tea she used to make.

'You need to boil the tea leaves long, and then only add milk. Adding milk early gives an uncooked taste,' she would always chirp in.

He said nothing today. When someone gets used to good things, it is no longer appreciated. The feeling of – 'I deserve it, so what?' grows strong.

'And how are things over there?' she asked.

'As usual, for the last two days, my maid is not turning up,' he wanted to say 'our maid', but then this is what came out of his mouth.

'They are just this way only. Here also, Najjo did not turn up yesterday. Anyway, how is the cold over there? Have you bought a heater or blower?' Devyani asked.

'Yes, I told you last week over phone, I bought a fan heater.'

'Oh yes, yes, I forgot. You go upstairs in my room and change. I have turned on the geyser, in case you want to freshen up. I'll bring the lunch upstairs.' Saying this Devyani went to the kitchen.

'Yes, you better relax, must be exhausted. It's a long way from Delhi. Relax son.' Aunty said.

Divaker went upstairs and changed into pyjama and kurta. The chill touched his whole leg, ankle to waist. The denim that he was wearing all the way kept the cold out, but it was not as comfortable. He jumped into the bed and pulled the quilt all over him. It was real good. He felt a new lease of life. Devyani pushed open the door after some time with her shoulder. She was holding a tray with plates, spoon and bowls.

'Shall I serve the lunch there?' she asked.

'Sure, I am as hungry as…as…as…' Divaker could not find words.

She giggled.

Something about her was so utterly genuine. She sat opposite to him on the bed and they both helped each other with the dishes. The smell of homemade food filled the whole room. Divaker does not get homemade food there in Delhi. His source of lunch is the office canteen, for breakfast and dinner; he had to depend on himself or Ammaji – the maid who works at his place. Therefore, this typical home lunch was a luxury for him.

'I always like few things that Aunty cooks,' Divaker said.

'I have made the dal and mutton stew, yes mummy helped me with the chapatti,' Devyani defended.

He looked at her with disbelief and she understood.

'Yes, I am just trying my hand out at cooking off lately. Nothing much to do, moreover, mummy is not feeling well these days,' Devyani clarified further.

After a sumptuous meal, she cleared away the plates, went downstairs and few minutes later came back. She sat beside him on the bed.

'How is your job going on?' Divaker asked.

'Boring, every morning I have to get up at seven or seven thirty, make breakfast, take a bath, get ready and leave home by nine' o clock. In the bank also, same people, same everyday stress, everything makes me believe that life has come to a standstill.'

Soon after a year of their marriage, she got a job with a nationalized bank. Average salary, but a lifetime secured job and post retirement pension made the offer lucrative. During the initial years of their relationship and before marriage, he was never in her favor of doing a job. The same old typical male sentiments accompanied with personal insecurity.

That time she was doing her masters in zoology. Later, the more he started understanding her, he realized the efforts she was putting to studies. Moreover, she was a bright student and always did well in exams. He also understood that getting her to do household chores would only waste her talent. She always wanted to prove her worth, not to him or anyone else, but to her parents because they never ever appreciated or understood the potential she had. In household similar to theirs, seldom do you find a girl who has done her masters in science.

The degree was not going to come to her naturally, and it took hours of study everyday and many sleepless nights. The nights turned out talk less also, as they used to avoid late night chatting on phone. Later, he changed his mind and started encouraging her for a professional career as well.

Devyani was sitting silently beside him now. He spread out the quilt on her legs, and she pulled it up to the waist. The room was little dark, and in the light of table lamp kept over the bedside shelf, Divaker saw her face. The face of a candid girl, whom he married few years back, had gradually turned to a women's face. He got close to her, held her beautiful face in his palms and kissed on the forehead.

'Don't worry, things will be okay, soon,' he said.

She buried herself more into the quilt and kept her head on Divaker's shoulder. He was caressing the long hairs and held her close to him strongly. It had been a long time that he had felt this warmth and tenderness, which always made him feel at home. Divaker was taking long breaths, and the scent of Devyani's body - feminine and personal - soon made him forget everything else.

2

The Soap Seller

It was dark outside when he woke up. Days become strangely short during winters. She was still lying beside him, eyes closed, like a child, dreaming and getting happy.

On times like this he often felt that how complete and satisfied his life is, having almost everything that he once dreamed of, and believed that one day God will definitely make his dreams come true.

He is an ordinary man with ordinary dreams, today and twelve years back also when he used to travel in DTC buses with a heavy bag on his shoulders – which most of the time did not even find a place on the floor of the bus – leave aside chances of Divaker getting a seat. The bag, full of detergent and room freshener, and people staring and cursing the bag for the space it occupied in the already packed bus. Divaker used to look away from them, pretending as if the bag did not belong to him.

This was Divaker twelve years back. Things have changed a lot over years, and it seems as if it was just the other day which passed by. Time just went by in a flash.

Twelve years back it was a sunny summer morning when he first set his foot on New Delhi railway station. He had few things with him, like – high school mark sheet, few clothes, a couple of thousand rupees, his destiny, and a dream of being admitted to a good college for graduation degree in commerce. It took less than a week for his dream to shatter. The respectable figures of mediocrity on his mark sheet could not even make his name appear in the third list of any of the colleges in north campus. Yes, his name appeared. His name appeared in the second list of a little known college in south campus. He could not take admission there also, and then he was enlightened by the fact that he could not have been able to take admission anywhere. Reason being, that the two thousand rupees in his bag was not enough to pay off even for a semester. His distant maternal uncle with whom he was staying – out of compulsion or formality offered help, but by that time, the realization of truth was so bitter, that he could not think otherwise.

It was for the first time that he had a rendezvous with the other side of life. It was the face of life, which is neither pleasing, nor beautiful. The face you have to see no matter how many times you turn away your eyes. It's like looking at a mirror which shows you different faces each time. Some of the faces were beautiful, some funny, some bad, some ugly, and some utterly disgusting. That was the time he entered manhood. He was no longer a kid or a teenager. He was a grown up man; a man with new difficulties, challenges, and failures, like a new more difficult stage of videogame. Divaker found himself fumbling with the game pad in his hands. That was the time he realized that life has started, his real life.

Indecisive and confused he kept on pondering what's going to happen next.

'Will I really miss my graduation degree admission?'

'Am I going to be a non graduate for the rest of my life?'

'What face do I have to show to everyone else, once I go back from Delhi to my place?'

'Everyone will blame my mediocre result.'

Above all Papa, who always used to call him an idiot and worthless fellow.

He kept on wondering and thinking over the possible consequences of not being able to get admission to the graduate degree course. He felt something revolting inside him. A voice within himself, asked him to break everything that is conventional and average.

'Why will everyone blame me?'

'I did study hard, what can I do, if I did not secure good marks?'

'What if I secured an A+ grade?'

'Did I have enough money to pay off my admission fee in a good college?'

But then, he was the person to be blamed, because he was on the other end of the problem.

Somebody came to his rescue and advised him to take admission in 'School of Correspondence and Continuing Education.' They will give a Delhi University degree and certificate. The University, as a part of the distant learning programme, ran it. There will be no classes, only study matter dispatched to you. Just appear for the exams on time. No classes, so less fee. The proposition appeared to be his passport and visa to a land, which seemed to be so far and unreachable. He filled up the form, affixed photograph and gave his maternal uncle's local address. He was now going to stay.

Everyday, he used to wait for the study material to arrive. He made tea and breakfast for himself and his uncle, who went to office everyday at eight thirty. Divaker would go through the newspaper, every word of it for two to three hours. The classified column was of main interest to him.

'Wanted sales exececutive.10+2. Good fluency in English & pleasing personality. Salary 2000 + D.A.'

'MNC bank looking for bright energetic person for direct selling of car finance schemes. 10+2 or Graduates need apply. Salary 3000+Incentive.'

'International home products Mfrg looking for dynamic, self motivated boys and girls for direct selling world class products. Salary no bar.

Something started to cook in his mind. He kept the lid closed and allowed it to simmer.

His uncle returned from office with a vacant and empty face every evening. He would lie down immediately after removing his shoes and close his eyes. Often he would take half an hour quick nap to refresh after a full days work. He was a government employee, at a good position, in some data maintenance department.

'Did it come today?' he started asking daily, as if indirectly putting forward, 'how long will you stay?'

'No, but it may come any day now,' Divaker would reply, and get back to his daily routine of making dinner for both of them.

His uncle was a solitary, silent, and God-fearing person. For the rest of the evening they hardly used to talk. Uncle watched TV, and Divaker used to make dinner. It was a small one-room apartment, so being in front of each other and not talking made Divaker feel awkward. Divaker felt as if his presence is irritating his uncle.

Divaker's uncle should have been married by now, he was somewhere around thirty-five. Divaker thought that everyone needs a companion at one point of time and not getting one makes a person burnt out, and depressed. Maybe his uncle too was going through same mental deprivation. Who knows?

And, Divaker was right.

Then one day the much-awaited parcel arrived. It was 2.5 kg bundle of most economically possible printed and bounded books. He sifted through eight or ten such books, and found that two books did not belong to commerce first year. It was perhaps mistakenly changed with a history bunch. No matter, he started his studies, followed the instructions on each chapter, and page by page he kept reading and doing the exercises.

Divaker skipped parts of the matter he did not understand hoping that he would get back to it once he understands the whole thing. In a weeks time he realized that it was not a jigsaw puzzle. It required a systemic understanding to understand the whole subject, especially accountancy. Really, there is no alternative to classroom, teachers, lectures and discussions. A single room apartment with a 2.5 kg bundle of books can never be a college, a university, a campus. He was filled with remorse and anger over things, which were beyond his control.

'Why does one go to college?'

'Why does one can't go to college because he has less marks or money?'

'Does everyone go to college for a job in future?'

'Is it necessary to have a job to earn money?'

'Are jobs only for those who go to good colleges?'

He felt his mind expanding beyond limits. He was asking questions to himself, which he never asked. He was thinking about things, which he never imagined. He was going to learn anyhow. He made up his mind to expand his horizon. He was going to learn from this world. Learning - not education - was his first priority.

In the evening, he told his Uncle that since he was going to stay there for long – maybe three years – he was rather thinking to find a separate accommodation for himself. Uncle readily agreed and helped him in finding a single set room, with a pre-existing occupant. This pre-existing occupant was the person with whom he was going to share his room and three very valuable years of his life. A life full of hardship, challenges, sweetness, joys, sorrows, hopes, dreams, despair, achievement and learning; they soon became great friends. His name was Gaurav.

Six months passed by and his second bunch of books arrived.

'I want to do some kind of a Job,' Divaker told Gaurav one day.

'What kind of a job?'

'Just anything that comes across, whatever.'

'You are only a high school pass, you will end up with some small time jobs and companies,' Gaurav said, concerned.

'See, I don't have to go to college to attend classes. I'm free all day. I want to use this time, earn some money. I know enough, about how much I need to study to pass the exams. Moreover, I do not want to be a university topper,' Divaker did not want to unfold his story once more to him. By that time, Gaurav was aware of everything that Divaker had been through recently. Gaurav understood and nodded. That day Divaker spent quite some time highlighting and underlining vacancies, released in the Times Classified columns.

'Great opportunity! Earn as much as you want! Be a part of a FMCG giant. 10+2/Grads. Good communication, go - getter, self-motivated. Fresher Welcome! Walk-in interviews at........'

Divaker was standing in front of a two-storey house, and

checked the address again from a paper cutting which he took out from his pocket. It was wet with sweat. Gaurav, in his old vespa scooter accompanied him.

'This must be the one,' Divaker said.

'Looks more like someone's house rather than an office,' Gaurav was right.

'Let's see.'

They walked past the gate. A flight of dark stairs led them to a dimly lit room. Almost two dozen faces stared, as soon as they entered. They were candidates for the interview just like Divaker. A cheaply dressed receptionist sat behind a small table at one corner near the door, which opened into another room where interviews were going on.

'Please take your seat and submit your resume,' the receptionist said with an expressionless face.

He gave a copy of the résumé and sat on one of the chairs, which were placed closely against the wall.

'All the best! We will meet in the evening.' Saying this Gaurav went to attend his own business. Divaker saw people going in and coming out of the room. He was a bit nervous for the first interview of his life. He prayed for his selection and patiently awaited his turn, remembering and summarizing few interview etiquettes, which he read in a Readers Digest some time back. In an hour, his name was called.

'May I come in Sir,' standing at the door he could see the other man – his interviewer – sitting behind a desk on the other side of the room.

'Yes, please,' an over-enthusiastic reply came.

He went inside the room and kept on standing for a while, remembering it's not polite to pull a chair until asked for.

'Please be seated Mr. Divaker Acharya.'

'Thank you, Sir.'

The man held his resume, and was going through it. He was a middle aged, dark, and a person of average physique. There was no sophistication in his body language, or in the way he dressed.

'Please tell me something about yourself?' he asked.

'Sir, my name is Divaker Acharya. I have done my matriculation from Vivekananda Vidyapeeth, Jasidih, Bihar. I secured.........'

'All that is already written in your resume,' he cut Divaker short, 'I want to know something which is not mentioned in your resume. Like ummm....., your strengths and weaknesses.'

'Okay Sir, sorry. My weakness is.........'

'Strengths first my friend,' the man again stopped Divaker.

He spoke English in a way as if he has recently been through a crash course on spoken English. In spite of all the stress in facing the interview, his mind could take out some time in analyzing the 'man behind the desk.'

'Sir, my strengths are that, I am hardworking, honest and ambitious. I am a dedicated person........'

'Dedicated to whom? Ha ha ha ha.......'

Divaker was sweating and stammering a bit. After a brief laugh, the interviewer was quite again and got back to what he was expected to do.

'Please continue,' he said, waving his hand a little.

'And my weakness is that I feel disheartened when my efforts are not recognized,' at that point of time, this was the only thing which came to mind, and jumped out of his mouth.

Divaker did not know many of his own weak points then. It is at a later stage of life that he started discovering himself. A certain level of mental maturity is required for self-analysis.

'Ummm...... that's true, very true. Tell me something about your hobbies and interest,' he asked.

'Sir, I like reading books, listening music, photography and poetry.'

'Poetry, good, do you write?'

'No Sir, I like reading,' he lied, had he asked Divaker to recite some of his own stuff, he could not have recalled a single line from any of those two diaries.

'Okay, let's see if you remember anything.'

Divaker recited a very common couplet of Mirza Ghalib, which anyone with a little touch of Urdu can understand.

'Good one, but what does it mean?' the man asked.

Divaker described its meaning.

'Wah! Wah! Kya khoob kaha hai,' he nodded his head a couple of times as if trying to absorb the whole thing in his head. 'You are a high-school pass, doing graduation by correspondence. Will you study or work?' he got back to the business and started going through his resume once more.

'Both Sir, I will work during day, at night and on holidays, I will study. Moreover, the course I am pursuing is not that demanding.' Divaker said.

This was a way, Divaker used to convince himself for the working option. It was an ammunition, which he used to fight against the voice from inside his heart, which asked him to study full time.

'Well, fine. Do you know anything about the job for which you are here?'

'No Sir, but would like to know.'

'Ok, we are a direct sales associate of a FMCG company dealing in detergents, toilet cleaner, room freshener, shampoos etc. We need salesperson for directly selling these goods door to door. Are you willing to join?'

Options are for those who have choices, and it definitely was not the case with him.

'Yes Sir, sure.'

'Ok, fine. Meet me day after tomorrow.'

'Am I selected Sir?' Divaker enquired doubtfully.

'Yes, send in the next one,' the man said in a loud voice enough for the receptionist sitting outside to hear.

He thought to ask about his salary as he was leaving the room, but did not. He tried to escape before the interviewer could change his mind. He did not talk to anyone outside. Everybody tried to read his face, and guess what probably happened in the interview. He gathered speed and flew down the stairs, out of the gate and then on the road. He looked back to see the house once more.

'I will ask about the salary day after tomorrow,' he said to himself.

'That's fine, but how much will they pay,' Gaurav asked perplexed. He was back in the room half an hour before Divaker returned in the evening, and listened to what happened throughout the day.

'I will come to know about it day after tomorrow.'

'But you should have asked about it.'

'Doesn't matter much, what matters is that I need to start somewhere and someday. It's already six months now. I normally complete the semester syllabus in three months time, up to my best possible extent. I need to take some sort of coaching to understand parts of the subject I have not understood. Last month I did not receive the money order Papa sends. Some problem at his end, maybe.' Divaker said a lot of things, and tried to answer certain questions which Gaurav tried to ask, but could not.

'Don't worry, it will come this month. Moreover, I am there, and this months rent is already paid,' Gaurav said, trying to look at things from Divaker's perspective, and in some way support him, in whatever possible way he could.

He was not looking forward to the money order. He remembered the monologue that he had with Papa over phone last month.

Use the money judiciously.

Do not overspend.

It's really very difficult to manage funds for you.

This time I had to borrow from a friend.

Papa never enquired about how his studies were going on. Yes, he used to ask about how he was managing lunch, dinner etc. Little did he know that one thousand five hundred rupees were not enough to survive in a place like Delhi. Divaker's contribution for the room rent was seven hundred fifty, same for Gaurav. A below standard meal at roadside hotel used to cost them fifteen rupees per head, that turns out to be nine hundred rupees per month, calculated at two meals per day. Where is money left? It's already deficit. Leave aside tea, breakfast, local bus fare, stationary, toiletries etc, and yes, much needed coaching classes also. Divaker understood Papa's problem. He never said anything. He understood that Papa did not get a salary revision for the last twelve years, while inflation has grown many folds in the same period. An average employee of a loss incurring public sector warehousing company could not manage more.

'What's up your mind?' Gaurav asked smiling, 'Now you have a job, it's a success day. Let's celebrate.'

They did not go to the roadside hotel for dinner. Instead went to a Chinese fast food joint, two blocks down the same road. They shared their problems, encouraged each other and had a very good time that evening. Gaurav also told about his latest girlfriend, with whom he was hanging around off lately. He used to earn well, from his artificial-flower-arrangements business. It was a one-man show. He bought artificial flowers at wholesale rates from an importer in Paharganj, got terracotta or ceramic vases from Shahadra, and wrought iron arrangements from Gandhinagar. He aesthetically selected flowers, fixed them on whatever best suited, or as per specifications with plaster-of-paris or vinyl glue, and off he was ready with a beautiful fake flower bouquet! Some of them even had fake dewdrops on them. He sold them to gift shops.

'I'll close this file by weekend,' Gaurav said ambitiously.

'What file?'

'That girl, Meenu, it took me a month to get along with her. Let her open up her legs and I'll better wind her up,' he smiled.

Everyone has a side of one's personality, which does not seem right to others. It happens with everyone. Previously Divaker used to think that Gaurav is not right, but when he had seen enough, he realized that overall there has been a significant fall in our values. Why should Gaurav be the only person to blame? He never made fake promises to anyone. Out there, if one is ready to be screwed, then why feel bad about the whole thing.

They were back to the room. Gaurav had to make some deliveries the day after, so he got down with flower arrangements. Divaker turned his face to the wall, lying on the single mattress. He was soon asleep.

The next day he washed and ironed his best pair of trouser and shirt. 'The man behind the desk' in a dim room has asked to report tomorrow. He felt as if he had grown up considerably. From tomorrow, he is going to start a career, a job, and he shall be earning. Maybe, he will send some money back home also. They'll be happy to know that he has started doing a job, when he'll inform them. But no, not now. Sometime later, maybe yes. The fear of unknown clipped his thought. The whole day went by in an anxious anticipation of how his life is going to take a turn. The day went by, and the night. He woke up; it was Monday morning.

'Also carry a notebook, maybe for the first few days they will take you through some product training kind of thing,' Gaurav suggested.

'Yes, I bought a folio yesterday, it has a notebook, pen, pad and a calculator,' he beamed back with a sense of satisfaction.

Divaker started off at eight' o clock next morning. After changing two local buses and walking for fifteen minutes, he was finally in front of the same house like office. It was nine thirty. Few well dressed, and few not so well dressed boys were already strolling near the gate.

'Did they ask you to report here today?' one of them asked Divaker.

'Yes,' Divaker said.

'Ok. We are also here to join today,' another one said, 'the office is not open yet. Therefore, we are waiting.'

Divaker recognized him as one of the blank faces staring at him on the interview day. He smiled. In the next half hour, another half a dozen boys joined their group. They all waited for the office to open. At ten thirty, 'the man behind the desk' appeared across the road. He greeted everybody and then went upstairs in the dark to open the office door. The group followed him. Inside it smelled damp, and foul. He opened a window to let in some fresh air.

'Please pull the chairs and be seated,' he said and went inside the other room. They all sat down in a classroom fashion. A couple of minutes later the man came back with a big black bag, and sat on the small chair, on which the receptionist girl was seated day before yesterday.

'I will tell something about the products,' he announced.

He groped his hand inside the bag and took it out, holding a bright-labeled plastic bottle.

'This is FLOOR MASTER, our flagship product. As the name suggests, it is a floor cleaner to be used two capfuls in half-bucket water. It disinfects and cleans floor. It is multipurpose, means that, FLOOR MASTER can also be used as toilet cleaner without dilution,' he completed.

'How much does it cost?' one of the boys asked.

'Good question! The price at which it is to be sold is eighty rupees. Also, we offer a free gift with every purchase,' he again groped inside the bag, and came out with a detergent bar.

'This is CHAMPION, another quality product, CHAMPION comes free with FLOOR MASTER,' the man said.

'What if someone wants to buy the soap and not the floor cleaner?' a boy in the group asked, who had been listening very attentively.

'Selling price of CHAMPION is rupees ten only. It can be sold separately also, but try to insist and sell four bars at the price of three. With three bars, one bar comes free.'

He again put his hand in the bag and came out with a spray can. Everyone's eyes followed his movements, and he came up with new things each time like a magician.

'This is MR. FRESH, our volume building product. MR.FRESH is basically a room freshener, but once sprayed it keeps out mosquitoes also. That's not written anywhere, if someone asks, say that this is a herbal stuff. Selling price is rupees one hundred twenty only,' he was now silent, and his eyes scanned through every face. Trying to read the impact his 'magic' had on them. Divaker hid himself behind the shoulder of a guy sitting in front of him.

Just then, three men entered the room and greeted the 'man behind the desk'. He responded and asked them to sit in the adjoining room. All of them went inside the other room. It seemed they were older guys of trade.

'We will be in action from today itself. Alright?' He asked in the tone of an army captain. The training was perhaps finished.

'What about salary and all?' Divaker could not make out from where in the group this voice came, but the question was relieving for him.

'Oh... yes,yes,' he was taken aback. But 'the man behind the desk' pretended as if the question is warmly welcomed.

'See, for fresher like you, we pay one thousand five hundred per month and a daily allowance of fifty rupees per working day. Of course! Once in field, you will make good money, as you start earning incentives also.' He confirmed everyone in a defensive tone as if he is aware of the fact that the salary is insufficient.

That is fine, Divaker thought, at least he can make another thousand rupees from incentives plus the daily allowance will take care of lunch and local bus tickets. In continuation with his thoughts, he suddenly asked, 'how much can we earn from incentives?'

'A good amount, your team leader will brief you all about it, once you are in the field. Let's not waste time sitting here, I will shortly introduce you to your team leader,' he went inside the other room and came back after ten minutes, with the other three men. They introduced themselves, and said that they had divided their whole group into three subgroups. Each of them will lead a group. They started calling their names in random. A short and stout fellow called Divaker's name, it means Divaker was in his team.

'We will work in East of Kailash colony today,' he addressed the whole team. They all surrounded him and listened to his instructions. They were a group of eight boys. He carried on, 'I will carry the main bag, and our base point will be East of Kailash community centre. Upon reaching there, you all will take stocks from me and start working. Once the stock in your hand is finished, you can get back to me for more stock.

They all took a local bus from the next street and in half an hour, they were in East of Kailash community centre. It was pathetic to see the short guy – their team leader – carrying a huge, heavy bag in the summer heat. He put down the bag from his shoulder in front of Nirulas restaurant. They again surrounded him like sheeps.

Everyone watched them, men, women, boys, girls, kids and everyone. People came in long cars, went inside the restaurant, and came out. Everyone watched them but paid no attention.

'Half of the day is gone,' he said, 'you will find me here for the remaining half.'

He took out a bunch of polythene bags and started putting goods in those bags.

'Two units each of Floor master, ten units of champion and two units each of Mr. Fresh,' he repeated the same line eight times, as he handed over the individual polythene bag to each one of them. He continued, 'In groups of two, you will all spread out in four directions. Today is training day; we will wind up at

5' o clock. I will meet you here. Meanwhile if you run out of your stocks get back and take more stocks from me. From tomorrow onwards, you all will get your individual bags. Best of luck, see you in the evening.'

They set forth. With Divaker was a boy with whom he had a little talk while coming to East of Kailash in the bus. Divaker knew his name and where he lived, he carried on the incomplete conversation.

'Who else in your family,' Divaker asked.

'Father, Mother, and three sisters.'

'You are the eldest?' Divaker probed further.

'Yes, I had an elder brother, two years back he expired in a road accident.'

Divaker felt bad about it, he was silent, but then his silence made the boy more uncomfortable.

'What does your father do?' Divaker asked.

'He is retired Border Security Force personnel,'

Divaker got a whole picture of his family. Divaker was not looking forward to the boy asking the same questions. He knew that his answers would not have been so brief and objective. Moreover, his answers would have compelled the boy to ask few more questions. He wanted to avoid such a situation.

'Should we start from this house?' Divaker asked, standing in front of a large house with black gate. The boy nodded. He pressed the doorbell, which was placed apart from the gate as if to keep visitors away. The gate clanked, and a peeping window opened within the gate. The gate did not open.

'Yes, what do you want?' the man at the peeping window asked sternly. They saw him wearing a uniform hat. This must be a security guard

'We are from DSL marketing. We deal in home products of everyday use. We just wanted.......,' he could not complete.

'No, no salesman,' saying this guard slammed the peeping window.

'It's not going to be easy. Isn't it?' Divaker was looking for some encouragement from his partner.

'That's true, before joining this place; I worked for a firm dealing in hosiery goods. The bag that I used to carry was no less than a sack. Here at least the bag is smaller.'

Divaker got his answer. The next gate was not as big as the first one. Here the gate opened.

'We are from DSL marketing...........may I have five minutes of your valuable time,' he could complete the introduction this time.

'Ok, show me the stuff you have.' their prospective customer replied.

'Sir, this is Floor Master.............and the best part is that you get a free detergent cake – Champion – with your purchase,' he was heaving with the excitement of being able to deliver his first sales call. His partner briefed the man about Mr. Fresh.

'How much for the floor cleaner?' their customer asked.

'Rupees eighty only Sir, with a champion detergent bar free,' he beamed back in excitement.

'Will you give it for forty?'

Divaker was taken aback. Nothing was told to them about discounts or bargaining. He did not know to handle. If he sells for less, maybe he had to pay the balance amount from his own pocket. He did not take chance.

'They do, salesman like you often give goods at a good bargain,' their customer convinced Divaker.

'No Sir, we can't sell at less than this price,' Divaker replied firmly, but disheartened.

'No problem, I was just enquiring. The owners are not here now. I am only a caretaker of this house.'

The 'customer' went inside, they gathered the goods back in the polythene bag, and walked down the porch.

'Don't leave the gate open,' a faint voice of the man came from somewhere deep inside the house.

'Ok Sir.'

They said nothing to each other. Divaker was disheartened, but his partner seemed perfectly all right. He perhaps knew what Divaker was thinking.

'It happens, you'll get used to it. This is your first exposure, maybe that's why you are feeling bad,' his partner said.

Divaker said nothing. They walked to the next gate. This was a duplex house. There was no bell. Divaker made a clanking sound at the gate, and they heard a furious barking of dogs from behind it. They took a step back. The gate remained closed.

'No, we don't want. Please go otherwise the dogs will keep on barking,' a female voice from any of the windows upstairs. No face. They moved on.

'You know, on an average; half a dozen sales men knock at their door everyday. It's obvious for anyone to get irritated,' Divaker's partner said.

'Yes, that's true. It's difficult to understand the problem of a person on the other side of things,' Divaker said.

He kept on repeating this line in his heart a number of times. Unknowingly and casually, he said something, which even today he says to people and himself also. Often unawares, people speak wisdom things. He did not know that this sentence is going to stay with him for a long time, maybe a lifetime. They moved to the next gate. By evening, they had knocked at almost fifty gates, a separate experience each time. Somewhere it was a matter of only few seconds, somewhere fifteen or twenty minutes. The taste of success after lot of failures was refreshing. He suddenly felt lighter, all the fatigue and exhaustion disappeared after each successful sales call.

By five o clock, they were able to sell the entire inventory given to them, except few bars of detergent.

'Should we turn back now?' his partner asked.

Divaker looked at his watch. It was five minutes to five.

'Better lets take a riksha, we have come up a long way knocking gates,' Divaker said with a tiresome face.

'If everyday we keep on taking riksha, our daily allowance of fifty rupees will not be enough,' his partner replied.

He smiled, his partner was right. Both of them started walking. It took them half an hour to reach the place from where they started.

'How was the day?' their team leader who had been standing like a statue, perhaps for the whole day asked. He was trying to figure out the stock left in the polythene bag.

'Fine, we almost sold the stock with us,' Divaker said, his voice lost its energy and he was trying hard to hide it.

'That's great! You must have learnt how it all works,' he looked straight into Divaker's eyes.

'Yeah, sure, I will do better tomorrow.'

'Yes, of course, definitely you have to do well,' the team leader said.

He took leftover stocks from all of them and put it in the big bag. More than half of the team members returned. The remaining joined one by one gradually, like soldiers returning from the front – exhausted, pale, sweating and smiling. It was a hot and humid day.

'So all back? We now return to the office,' the team leader announced and hanged the big bag over his shoulder.

Off they moved just the way they came. A local bus dropped them on a street next to the house like office. It was a similar day for all of them. The 'man behind the desk' took a group feedback from all of them. The girl at her small table was in her place this time.

'You all will get your areas today,' the man behind the desk said.

He called each one of them in the other room and allotted their specific area of operation.

'You are a newcomer to the city,' he said, when Divaker went inside, 'and putting up in Transyamuna. You go work in Mayur Vihar. Good residential colony.'

'Ok Sir,' he said.

'We expect a business of thirty thousand from your area every month to begin with,' he then added, 'above the sale of thirty thousand you get an incentive of five percent on the surplus amount.'

- 'Thank you Sir, Divaker understood that it meant selling goods worth rupees one thousand every day.

'Come to the office at nine AM tomorrow; take your bag and stock. Every evening you need to return the unsold goods and settle your account for the day. This is how we work.'

'Ok Sir, I will be here tomorrow morning at nine.'

It took Divaker one and a half hour to reach room.

'How was your first day at job?' Gaurav asked.

'Ok,' he replied.

'What's it like? means umm.... the job profile?'

'It's like, going door to door selling detergent and floor cleaner.'

'Is it a salesman job?' Gaurav looked at Divaker enquiringly.

'Yes, I knew, it's that only. Why? What you thought about it?'

'Well, I understood that it's a sales job, but then, I thought you may be calling upon a pre specified set of customers, or maybe some general stores. But this.....this I never thought. Anyway, as you say one needs to start somewhere and someday. How much will they pay?' Gaurav tried hard to conceal his disappointment.

'One thousand five hundred rupees per month, fifty rupees daily allowance per working day and incentives.'

Gaurav did not say anything, nor did he ask about the incentives. Overall, he was not much happy with the type of job proposition his friend got involved. They had dinner at the roadside hotel. They did not talk much. Divaker was exhausted; he slept early that night.

By seven thirty, Divaker left the room next morning. Gaurav just opened his eyes to say goodbye, and then rolled over the mattress again. Divaker thought he will have breakfast at some roadside hotel, but did not get time.

'Your bag is ready with stocks in it. Ten units each of Mr. Fresh and Floor master. Twenty units of Champion,' the girl at the small table probably arrived early today. A couple of boys were checking the stocks in their respective bags. Divaker signed a photocopied paper, as acknowledgement of goods received.

'All the best,' the girl said mechanically without looking at him.

'Thanks,' he said without looking at her.

He hung the bag on shoulders; just the way their team leader hung it yesterday and pushed off. A total sale for the day was around rupees seven hundred. He felt the money time and again in his pocket to see if it was there.

'How was the day?' the 'man behind the desk' asked when he came to return the unsold goods and settle accounts for the day. As he was talking, he continuously watched the bag, trying to figure out how much weight it has lost. God should have given these people something like x-ray vision.

'Fine, sold goods worth seven hundred,' Divaker said.

'Not bad, in fact good.'

He handed over to him seven hundred sixty rupees – revenue for the day, wrote down the details on the same photocopied paper, which he signed that morning. When Divaker was coming down the stairs, he saw his last day partner returning.

'How was it today?' the boy enquired.

'Not bad, in fact good,' Divaker replied.

It was eight o' clock in the evening when Divaker sopened the lock of his room. They had two keys, one with him, and the other with Gaurav. He was not back yet. Divaker's shirt was stinking of sweat. He did not have too many clothes. He washed the used clothes and undergarments, took a quick bath and walked down to the roadside hotel. Generally, they always had dinner together, but he could not control his hunger that time, although he felt guilty for not being able to wait for Gaurav. He ate to his hearts content. His eyes closed as soon as he straightened on mattress. Next morning he woke up and found Gaurav fast asleep. He had no idea when Gaurav came back last night.

Life went on like this for another six months. Divaker had become used to traveling in local buses with crowd, sweat and his bag. The bundle of study material had gathered a lot of dust. His first year examination schedule was released. He sifted through the pages of study material one Sunday; it smelled of fresh paper and print.

'Sir, I want to take a long leave,' he said to his boss – the man behind the desk – next Monday.

'What for? How many days?' he enquired irritatingly.

'A month, or forty five days maybe. My examinations will be starting by month end.'

He looked tensed and took some time to answer Divaker.

'See, we don't have anything called long leave, it's a small business that we are running. We can't afford giving people long leaves. No matter how important it maybe,' his boss said.

'But Sir, I can't afford to miss my first year exams,' Divaker bounced back in surprise.

'Yes, exam is also important. What I can do is settle your account until date. You give your exams. Once you are through, you can again come back and start all over.'

He had worked for twelve days that month. The 'man behind the desk' paid him twelve hundred rupees by cash, including his daily allowance. He signed on a revenue stamp. That was the last time Divaker ever saw 'the man behind the desk', that house like office, that girl with her small table and that big bag he used to carry.

In those six months, he had a fairly good idea about life and this world we live in. Earning money is not as easy job. Having knocked at around five thousand doors, seen different people, interacted with few thousand of them, he had an understanding of people, events and his position in this big big world. It was only once that he earned an incentive of thousand rupees. Divaker could never start the much-needed coaching classes, but yes, there was improvement in his quality of life. He never asked Papa for money. For the last two months, he did not again receive the money order. Papa did not call up, nor did he call up. It was almost a month. He will have some time once exams are over. He would better visit people back home.

He started turning pages of the study material, which were never turned. With only twenty days to go for the first exam, Divaker could spend no time trying to understand things he did not. Things not understood are to be skipped over. He had to finish off the syllabus as early as possible. He was stressed, but he had no repentance for not being able to study for the last few months. He knew that he had to finish it off somehow. Exams started, and he appeared in all of them. A duty, which had to be done, somehow.

3

The Road by the River

Exams over, Divaker went home (no, not home, 'home' and 'house' are two different things, they mean different feelings) for a week, forty hours of journey by train, and three hours of journey by bus. Papa was posted in a small town of Assam. His sister – Misty – stayed with Papa. Maa lived with her parents four hundred miles away in a remote village of Bengal. Divaker stayed for three days with Papa and Misty, and then moved on to meet Maa. His journey back to Delhi was scheduled from there. The whole week was a week of nostalgia and realization. He had a great time, especially with Misty and their dog. It occurred in his mind to tell them about the job, but he did not.

'Get me out of here one day when you start earning well and stand on your own feet,' Maa said with tears in her eyes.

Divaker did not say a word but he put his hand on her shoulder and she wept.

'Yes, I will. Don't worry. Take care. I will come back soon,' he could say only this much.

He started back his journey to Delhi. From that, remote village of Bengal he walked for an hour on the brick leveled road amongst lush green paddy fields. Someone was helping him carry the suitcase on a cycle. The air was clean and fresh. Everything was so silent that he heard the breeze flowing gently on the face. For that one hour, he saw only a few people on the road – farmers carrying jute on their bicycle. Really, this world is huge. He has a long way to go, and he did not have much time in hands. He needs to do things fast, real fast, but how? Divaker reached the pukka road, and the man helping him untied the suitcase from his cycle. This road was a narrow stretch of asphalt, with more potholes than asphalt.

'The bus will be coming from this way,' the man said in broken Bangla, and pointed to a direction where the road winded and disappeared in the trees.

'Yes, I know. I come here almost every year,' Divaker said, and handed over a ten-rupee note to him, 'have some tea biscuit.'

The man was more than happy. He hurriedly rode his cycle and disappeared somewhere in the paddy fields as if the note will vanish if he stayed there for long. Simple mind, happy life. We unnecessarily complicate our life with our own set of complex thinking. But then, we are so used to complex thought process that we can't think otherwise. Even if we want, the world and its people will not allow us to think of life in simpler terms. Divaker imagined someone else giving him a ten-rupee note and saying, 'have some tea biscuit.'

He was horrified.

Three hours of journey on a wooden seat of bus which never crossed twenty-five mph, left him stirred when he reached the railway station. He had two hours in hand, so he decided to have dinner at the railway canteen. It was already eleven PM, when he boarded the train. Next morning he was crossing Bihar. The same evening the train entered Uttar Pradesh, and then the second morning he was entering Delhi. Divaker felt as if whatever happened last week was a dream. Papa, Misty, Maa, their dog, paddy fields, farmer on cycle; everything ran in his mind like flashes from a dream. He was back to Delhi to wait for the results and make way for his destiny.

Gaurav was still sleeping when he reached the room; he opened the door with sleepy and half-closed eyes.

'Come,' was all that he could say. He again thumped on the mattress. Divaker went to bathroom. When he came out, he saw Gaurav sleeping in a different posture.

'What have you brought for me?' Gaurav demanded, in a voice, which made Divaker feel as if he was talking in his dreams.

'Chane ka halwa.'

'Very good, take it out,' Gaurav got up from the mattress, and headed straight for the bathroom.

They were both fond of food. They had breakfast together after quite a long time. Gaurav ate a plentiful of halwa, which Maa made for hours on wood fire.

'How is everyone at home?' he was out of his sleep lag by now.

'Fine, everyone back there knows you now. They enquired about you too.'

'Okay, what's in your mind now? When will your results come?'

'Still a month's time for results to come. I will get back to some work meanwhile.'

'Again the same.....,' Gaurav was about to ask something.

'I know, not the same again. I will do something else now.'

'You know, I never said this thing to you, but I was never happy with your decision to take up that job. I never said this, I was afraid you may feel bad,' Gaurav said honestly.

'I understand, but nothing in life goes waste. I will try to find out something better for me, don't worry.'

Gaurav later told Divaker that while he was away, he brought a girl to the room almost everyday, and had a fabulous time.

'Whom?' Divaker asked.

'Gudiya, ground floor, next block,' and he laughed hysterically. He was just mad for new girls, to go to bed with him. Even a house-maid would be okay; in times of need.

Divaker had seen this girl a number of times, on his way to the roadside hotel. Gaurav told him about her earlier also. However, Divaker never thought that the matter would stretch this far. She was an innocent looking sweet girl, whom anyone may propose or offer to marry. He felt disgusted about her.

Everyone has a past. Gaurav came to Delhi three years back, from a small village of western Uttar Pradesh. He did not come to study or pursue a career. He was rather forced to come, when one moonlit night he was caught red handed, with a carpenter's girl in his village. He came to Delhi wearing pyjama, and he stayed with a friend who belonged to the same village. His friend managed to get him a job in a gift shop, as counter salesman. Gaurav worked in that shop for about a year. He understood the market of gift items; manufacturing, distribution, profit margins etc. Soon he himself started making artificial flower bouquets for the shop he worked. Later, as demand picked up, he started to supplies to other shops in the same market, and later to shops in different markets. He bought a used vespa scooter to help him in his work. Business was growing, and at that time, he met Divaker.

It does not bother Divaker whatever his past had been. He was a great friend, a good person in terms of cooperation and support. Above all, Divaker learned a lot of things from him.

'Good, well,' and Divaker also laughed.

He did not waste much time that day. After breakfast, Divaker went to the nearby market and bought one copy each of two leading newspapers. He browsed quickly through the classified columns. By that time, he knew that what type of ads mean what type of job. He understood pretty well that he was not going to get a managerial job but then, he was now in a position to make choices, with his little experience. He underlined a modest ad – inviting young candidates with some experience to join a multinational bank in car finance business.

They were looking for sales executives to sell their car finance schemes. They did not mention anything about educational qualification. Divaker appeared for the interview next day. Here the office looked like an office, and he felt happy with the prospect of being able to work with a big name and a professional environment. The whole office was air-conditioned and silent. He became more conscious and felt that his clothes, shoes, and overall get-up were not up to the mark.

Anyhow, let's see; he said to himself. He was called in a cabin where two well-dressed men took the interview. They asked a lot of question about him, his family, educational qualification, career interest, previous job experience and things like that.

'How will you manage your job and studies?' one of them asked.

'Sir, I already have worked for six months and studied also, based on that experience I feel that I can pursue a professional career along with my studies,' Divaker replied.

When environment and people around change, the personality quickly adopts itself to the new situation most of the time. Divaker's body language and attitude seemed much more sophisticated to him, as compared to the previous interview, as if a different person inside him was doing all this.

'How satisfactory was your experience with ....,' one of them searched back into his resume.

'........DSL Marketing,' the other one completed looking into his resume.

'It was more of a learning experience for me. I worked as a grass root sales person, and that's what really matters. Although I did not earn well, but yes, the experience that I gained is invaluable and will remain with me for a lifetime,' Divaker said.

'Well do you know anything about the car finance business?'

'No Sir, not much. I only know that I have to sell the finance schemes designed by the company, and since there are other players in the market, the advantage your scheme offers has to be the main selling point.'

They looked at each other and seemed satisfied. Divaker sat erect with hands on his lap. His palms were sweating.

'One last question,' the person wearing specs continued, 'will you be able to sell car finance schemes?'

'Yes Sir, sure. I have sold detergents and floor cleaner of an unknown company, and I was good at that. I can definitely sell your car finance schemes.'

'Thank you, Mr. Divaker. Please be seated in the lobby, we will let you know shortly,' the specs guy said.

Divaker sat in the reception area, his heart pounding and mind racing with lots of question –

'Are they going to take me?'

'What are the things I did well in the interview?'

'Where could I have done even a better job?'

'What if they don't take me?'

'If not, tomorrow I have to appear for the interview at Nehru Place.'

'Should I tell about this job to everyone at home?'

'Yes.'

'No.'

'Maybe yes.'

After ten minutes, one of them called him. He went back to the cabin once more.

'Mr. Divaker, you are selected,' the man wearing specs said smiling.

'Oh! Thank you Sir,' he felt relieved.

'Since the bank does not hire employees at your position, we have few associates to serve the purpose. We have such an associate called Logos Finmart. You will be working with them. Your salary will come from them. But yes, for trainings, meetings and other such purposes you will have to come here,' the other one said.

'Ok, fine Sir,' Divaker was a bit disheartened.

'This is the address of Logos Finmart. You may contact them immediately, and get your appointment letter. They will also brief you about the training programme. Thank you.'

Divaker walked out of the cabin holding a card.

'This is what they call man power outsourcing. They need my work, but not me,' he thought.

He read the address of Logos Finmart. It was just two blocks away. He decided to go there immediately. It was a small office in a good commercial area, and had a professional environment. People were moving out with files, folio and bags. Posters and calendars of cars were hung on almost every wall. A group was having some sort of a discussion in the main room – there were three cabins with glass door.

'Yes, how may I help you,' somebody from the group asked, seeing Divakers enter the office.

'I am Divaker Acharya, and I have been selected for the vacancies released in yesterday's newspaper. I have come straight from the office after my interview.'

'Ok...ok...yes. Divaker Acharya, yes. They called up, and we were expecting you. By the way, I am Harvinder Saluja. You may call me Harry; everyone calls me by this name. I am one of the partners managing this business. We were just discussing what car finance business is like. These guys are your colleague,' he said pointing to the group,' they have also just joined in yesterday. I called up everyone today to have a little talk, know each other, and understand a bit about the basics too. After all, we all will be working together. Come join in.' a man of mid forties said.

Divaker gave a brief self-introduction to everyone and Harry introduced everyone in the group to Divaker. He pulled a chair and joined the group. Harry was a warm and enthusiastic man. Despite his age, he easily blended well with the young team he was working with. He had a good sense of humor. Divaker felt better with the idea of working with him.

'You all will have your formal training programme for three days starting tomorrow. Venue is the training room at bank premises, and time nine o' clock sharp in the morning,' Harry said to everyone.

Divaker joined their informal discussion, listened more and talked less. Two of them were fresher, four had some experience in different trades – like him – and two of them had already some exposure into car finance business, with some other bank. He gathered from the interaction that this was a highly competitive market, fluctuation of interest rates had a direct and immediate impact on business and in fact, nobody had an edge over others. They were free at about five o' clock.

'Sir, what about my appointment letter?' he asked Harry when everyone was leaving, 'they said in the bank that I will get it today.'

'Oh yes, I got it typed during the day, come,' Harry took him to a cabin.

Harry opened a cabinet and handed over a white envelope with 'LOGOS FINMART' printed in left corner. On a single sheet of letterhead his appointment letter was typed – the first appointment letter of Divaker's life.

'Thank you Sir,' his said and turned back to leave.

'See you tomorrow morning, be on time.'

'Ok Sir, sure.'

Divaker came back to his room, ironed his clothes, and polished shoes in preparation of tomorrows training programme.

'So, you got the job,' Gaurav said when they were having dinner at the roadside hotel, 'how much salary?'

'They will pay three thousand per month, and a petrol allowance of fifty rupees daily.' Divaker replied.

'Good, it's far better than the previous one.'

'Hmmm... right. I think now I shall tell everyone at home about the job. No, not now, let me work for some time.'

From next day his training started. Morning nine till seven in the evening with lunch breaks of one hour in between and other five minutes breaks. They were a group of nine boys. Harry used to sit with them but he would often vanish for hours together. After all, he was not a trainee like them. He must have attended such training programme a number of times. The bank people took up the sessions.

'We have the lowest rate of interest these days, and in last three months we have disbursed the maximum number of cases,' the sales manager said.

'But the bank I was working with also offers the same,' one of the experienced colleague said.

'Yes, that's true, but again they charge two thousand rupees processing fee per case from their customers. We do not do that. Maybe in future, if we bring down our rates, we may start charging. This is the scenario as of now, tomorrow it may change, but yes, we have to do business even then.'

The second day session on paper formalities and documentation was going on.

'You need to generate cases and give it to your associate. Your associate will pass these cases to us. We will see the documentation, and decide whether to approve loan to the party or not. All this may take two to three working days,' the trainer said.

'Suppose I generate ten cases, five of them are approved. Will I get credit for ten or five?' Divaker asked.

'You get credit only for approved cases. Yes, it doesn't matter whether it's a Mercedes or a Maruti.'

The three-day training was soon over. Harry wanted each one of them to get at least ten cases per month. Ten approved cases from anywhere. Divaker started fieldwork from the very next day, shop to shop, office to office. The training people had told them how to calculate monthly installment from the loan amount in a specific period. What were the documents required from an applicant and various other things which soon became a part of Divakers vocabulary. On an average day, he used to detail these things to at least twenty people. The fundamental were similar to selling detergents, but he was enjoying this job. As compared to a detergent salesman, here he found that more people paid attention to the product he was selling. Ever since a child, Divaker loved cars. His friends would tear magazine photographs of cars, show him the torn piece of paper and ask,

'What car is this?'

'Maruti 800 deluxe,' up came the reply.

'What car is this?'

'The grille looks like a Ford,' he replied confidently.

Here, he had to go to car showrooms often to give some paper or collect post-dated cheques. The sight of beautiful brand new cars moved Divaker. He tried to absorb the picture in best possible detail. He thought;

'How would the wheel feel like in this car?'

'They say the Aircon is fabulous. How comfortable will it be, when turned on.'

'This car is eighty two bhp, how much power does it mean?'

'The gearshift is chunky. It must be fun driving.'

He did not know driving, but he visualized himself driving with his family, enjoying life and having ice cream at India Gate after dinner. Devyani was nowhere in the picture that time, but he visualized a face, as wife, sitting at the seat beside him. His imaginary wife kept on changing faces as he kept on changing his imaginary cars. No taxes for dreaming. Once in a road show, he had a chance to sit in a newly launched Opel Astra. For the first time in life, he experienced the comfort of traveling in an air-conditioned vehicle.

His first year results came. He had scored a little over sixty percent. Average studies, average result, and average person. No, he was not an average person. He was growing intellectually. He had dreams and goals, long terms and short term. There is something called 'destiny', he knew that. This life is like a river, no matter whether you move or not, it will keep on flowing. It will flow past mountains, valleys, bridges, buildings, towns, villages and lush green paddy fields. The farmer with his bicycle will watch if flow. The river has to do a lot of things, and see a lot of things before it loses its existence.

He had a talk with Papa over phone that night.

'The results are out,' Divaker said.

'How much did you get?' Papa asked.

'Around sixty percent aggregate.'

'What around? What's your exact number?' he asked irritated.

'60.8 %.'

He was silent for some time.

'God knows what you will do with these marks. After spending so much money, this is what one has to see.' Papa was literally fuming with anger.

Divaker kept his mouth shut.

'Have you taken admission in second year yet?' Papa enquired, taking stock of the situation.

'Not yet, the fee for second year has to be paid, still seven days to left.'

'Ok, yes, yes. The fee has to be paid. How much?'

'Two thousand.'

'I gave you one thousand five hundred, when you came here. How much is left with you?' Papa asked, as if he had given an eternal cash box to spend money time to time, and just keep on updating the balance.

'Three or four hundred.'

'Again uncertain, will that time ever come when you will be sure of things,' a brief pause, and then with anger and disgust he said, 'careless fellow.'

Divaker kept the earpiece a little away from his ear, to understand only what he said, and to keep his anger and frustration away from him. Papa in fact expected to listen something from Divaker's side also. It would have given him an opportunity to expel out his frustration and hopelessness, but Divaker did not say a single thing. After some time Papa calmed down a bit. Divaker imagined the changing expression of his face, the bitterness draining out of his face gradually. Papa said, 'Okay. I will dispatch you two thousand rupees as early as possible.'

The whole conversation took a different turn, and Divaker was not prepared for it. He could say nothing about his job that time, although he had made up his mind of telling Papa about it.

Two days later, he got his first month salary at Logos Finmart. He went straight to the 'School of Correspondence and Continuing Education,' filled up the admission form for 2nd year commerce, and deposited the fees by cash. He did the same thing one year back, but then, there is a world of difference in this time gap of one year. Divaker felt more confident and secure.

'Knowledge and money is one's strength,' he said to himself, and took a long breath.

The money order of two thousand rupees arrived a week later. He paid off the rent. Divakers friendship with Gaurav had become stronger in one year of togetherness. They continued going to the same roadside hotel. Gaurav returned that evening after four days. Divaker had been using his scooter when Gaurav was out.

'Your scooter really helped me a lot,' Divaker said over dinner the same evening.

'In any metro city, having a means of conveyance is a necessity. It's not that.everyone needs a car, but yes, even a scooter serves the purpose.' Gaurav agreed.

'Yeah, that's true. I myself felt that my efficiency increased, and having a vehicle reduced my worries over small irritating things like waiting for local buses, sweat and crowd inside the buses. Moreover, I feel that I may need a scooter or motorcycle very soon. My mobility at job is increasing day by day. I need to touch more people and places every passing day,' Divaker said.

'Whatever you do, never buy a used vehicle. It's better to wait, but get a new one,' Gaurav suggested.

'Anyway, what are the prospects in nearby towns you went? Did anyone show interest in the samples you carried?'

'Yes, there are quite a few good shops in Aligarh, Agra and Meerut, but the problem is that they want a credit of more than a month. I don't have deep pockets, I run my business hand to ass. It involves risk also, in case my payment do not come on time, I will be stuck. But yes, there is a good market with opportunities, and people are doing good business. As of now I can't think on those lines; nobody knows what tomorrow holds for me,' he smiled and washed his hands after a satisfying meal.

'Good things happen to good people. Don't worry, its only a matter of time,' Divaker also washed his hand.

On their way back Gaurav said that, he saw a new hotel on the road running east of their colony. They were fed of the same food and same place. It was more than year. They both wanted a change.

'They charge eighteen rupees per meal, but the food is good; somebody told me a few days back,' Gaurav said.

'Ok, fine. Tomorrow we will have dinner there,' Gaurav supported.

That was the last time they had dinner at their pet roadside hotel. From next day, and then for almost a whole year, they both changed their dining address.

In a months time the bundle of study material arrived, for the first semester of second year. Divaker could unpack the parcel only on a Sunday. This was his second month at Logos Finmart. Last month he did a business of five cases.

'Pretty good way to start your innings! Next month do ten,' Harry said when they closed the last month sales. Two boys in the team did ten and eleven cases. Rest of them were almost at par with Divaker. Two boys could not do a single case. This month right from the start he felt the pressure of sales building upon him. Harry would daily follow-up with each one of them-

'What's up guys?'

'Anything new today?'

'What happened to your Ford Escort case?'

'Half of this month is gone, where are you all going to land?'

In this half months time Divaker could do only two cases. Although he brought in the highest number of applications, but only two got approved.

'Are you going to do less than what you did last month?' Harry asked him one day.

'No Sir, we still have fifteen days to go, and I have few very promising applications with me,' Divaker replied.

'Ok, well. I have very high expectations from you.'

Divaker tried to squeeze out the maximum possible from every minute of the day, but then there was a limit to what he could do. He often came across stuff like -

'Please pick up my documents from Malviya Nagar.'

'I remain busy during the day; meet me in the evening at my home in Rohini. I would better take my wife's opinion on which model to buy.'

'I don't need a car; my friend in Kirti Nagar needs a car loan. Take his address. You had better talk to him.'

These were some practical modalities of Divaker's job. His need to travel was increasing day by day, so was the pressure of results from him. In spite of running whole day here and there, by evening, he could finish only half of what he planned that morning. Much of his time was wasted in traveling. A local bus takes one hour to reach Rohini from Paharganj or Malviya Nagar from Rohini, and in some cases even an hour and a half. Leave aside the time wasted in searching the address; walking all the way. Taking a riksha for such sundry things would increase his daily expenses by more than a hundred rupees, which he could not manage in his daily allowance. All the boys in his team were local, from Delhi. All of them had a vehicle; whatever it was, scooter, bike or even a moped. But they had wheels of their own.

'Yes that's true, I understand because I had been through the same thing also,' Gaurav said.

Divaker discussed the problem with him one day.

'If it's a successful day, no matter how hard I wok, I remain fresh and energetic throughout the day, but these days when I see things going out of my hand, I feel irritated right in the morning,' Divaker said.

'It happened with me also. In my initial days, I used to carry my deliveries in bus. Half of my stuff got crushed or damaged, in the push and pull of the crowd in these stupid local buses. I was desperately in need of a scooter. In urgency I bought this second hand scooter and you know that this junk makes me weep everyday now.'

Divaker knew that Gaurav bought that used vespa scooter for ten thousand rupees. Gaurav did not have enough money and he had to borrow from Titu – the shop owner, Gaurav worked for – at monthly installments of three percent. It's almost a year and Gaurav was still paying back the money.

'Will anyone lend me some money?' Divaker asked, and he knew the answer as well. It's just that he wanted to hear it from someone else to convince himself.

'You are new to this place. You don't have enough contacts. Titu helped me because I was working in his shop and he knew that I could go nowhere. I still owe him some money, so I cannot go to him again. There are lots of other people I know but not a single one of them can bring out eight or ten thousand cash out of their wallet. Otherwise, what about your Uncle? He is in a government job, and earns well.' Gaurav said.

'No doubt he earns well, but one needs to have a bigger heart to help someone, not a bigger wallet. If I go to him the next thing we would ask is that why don't I ask from Papa. You know the whole matter, but I just can't narrate the whole thing to anyone only because I am in need of some cash.'

'Your office people?' he reminded Divaker.

'It's not even a couple of months that they know me. Do you think they will trust me?'

'No, but they are into car finance business. They must know any two-wheeler financer as well.'

'No one give finance to buy old vehicle, that too an old scooter.'

'Who said you need to buy an old scooter. Go for a brand new. Learn something from me. Every other day you find me at a mechanics shop. I spend more than five hundred rupees every month to keep it running. Do you want to be stuck at a repair shop and waste whole day half a dozen times every month? Your monthly installment will be around twelve hundred, if you buy the model which I have, and on the other hand you will save on your bus tickets and riksha fare.'

Gaurav was right. Divaker could see a silver lining now.

'No bank will finance your loan; you already know the documentation process. Things, which are required like residential proof, local address proof like phone bill or electricity bill, local guarantor having property in his name, bank statement for six months etc. No bank will approve your case,' Harry said, 'but I know few private financers who can do, but they charge a higher interest. I will talk and let you know.'

Two days later Harry got back to him,' your problem is solved. They are ready to give you a loan for seventy percent of the vehicle cost. I am taking your guarantee. They will give you twenty thousand, rest ten thousand you have to give as down payment, plus registration, insurance and road tax, another three thousand.'

'Ok, thank you Sir. I will take your help as soon as I am in a position to buy,' Divaker knew that his problem is still unsolved.

The thought of calling up Papa and telling him everything came to his mind. He called him in the evening.

'You got the money order?' Papa asked.

'Yes.'

'How is everything going on?'

'Fine, I got a job off lately.'

'Good, very good. What kind of a job is it? How much salary are they going to pay?'

'It's in a bank, car finance, three thousand, plus daily allowance.'

'That's good. I am very happy. However, don't compromise on your studies. That is also very important,' Papa gave some advice.

He expected Papa to show concern over the job. He expected Papa to ask him the reason of taking up a job, when his primary purpose of going Delhi was studies. Nothing of that sort happened. In contrary, Papa was happy, perhaps he felt relieved over the matter of sending money to him. Divaker tried hard to tell everything about his problem, his urgent need to buy a scooter, his need to travel around seventy-eighty miles everyday within the city. He could not.

'How is Misty?' Divaker asked.

'She is alright, vacation going on these days.'

'Okay, please take care. Bye.'

'Bye, you too take care.'

He hung up. The problem now seemed graver. The silver lining that appeared for some time soon vanished.

It was closing day. That month Divaker managed to get three more cases, five cases again this month.

'You need to pull up,' Harry said, 'other guys did fairly well as compared to last month.'

'Yes Sir.'

'Try and see if you can pull up to twelve cases next month.'

'Sure Sir.'

Divaker silently walked out of his cabin. He was putting in almost fourteen hours everyday, but his performance did not improve. He was depressed and felt sick when he got back to the room. Also, he did not talk much with Gaurav and slept early.

Weeks went by and then few months. His scooter dream never became a reality.

'What about your scooter? Are you buying it or not?' Harry asked him one day coming out of the toilet.

'Yes, I will buy, soon,' Divaker said smiling.

Harry never asked about it again and Divaker never mentioned about it to anyone.

4

Study Again .....

It was festival time, Diwali. Papa and Misty were expecting him at home during the holidays. He could not go. That month, Divaker did ten cases for the first time. In Diwali, People buy things they plan for during the year. Business boomed that month. The festival night he called up Papa.

'Wish you a very happy Diwali,' Divaker greeted him.

'Happy Diwali to you also, we are missing you,'

'Yes, I know. I too am missing you people a lot.'

'You could have come down, maybe for couple of days.'

'I wanted to, but could not manage. Lot of work to do here,' Divaker said.

Divaker wanted to say that; yes, he could have come down, had he received the money order for the last three months, he could have managed. However, he did not say anything.

'Yes, I understand. You can't imagine my relief, after you got the job. I told about it to my colleagues and friends. Everyone in my circle appreciated,' Papa said.

'Ok, Nothing more today. I don't have enough money this time. Happy Diwali once more.' Divaker said and hung up.

After he got this job and informed Papa, only once did he receive money from him. For months, he was managing everything on his own. On occasions, he felt pity on Papa and at times, the insensitivity that Diavker had to face made him furious. No matter what went inside his heart, he was always inert in his reactions. Never did he express anything. He was an idiot and worthless fellow, a donkey with an expressionless face. He wanted to go home, meet Misty, Maa and Papa too. He wanted to play with his dog. Going home means two thousand rupees, with all expenses paid. He was hardly left with any money at month end. The present scenario made it impossible to think about it even.

He called up Maa soon after talking to Papa.

'Happy Diwali Maa!' Divaker greeted her.

'Happy Diwali to you also Beta,' she started sobbing.

'Don't weep Maa, please don't weep. It's festival today.'

'I don't know any festival for the last ten years,' her sobbing increased.

He waited for a minute and she calmed down.

'Why didn't you come? Nana, Nani, Mamaji and everyone expected you.' Maa asked.

'Lot of work to do here Maa. New job, you understand.'

'Yes Beta, I understand. Do well in your job. Also, save some money. Without money nothing happens.'

'Yes Maa, I am trying to save.'

Divaker was in no mood to open up his pandora's box of troubles. She believed that one day, Divaker would be a great man type of thing, he would do some respectable job, earn well and bring her along to stay with him. A woman married for more than twenty years, and staying with her parents for the last five years, had nothing left with her except hopes.

'Yes, I know, you are a responsible child. See how early you have started earning. Boys of your age loiter here and there, but my son has started to earn,' she was happy now.

He felt good at being able to bring back smile on her face. She did not know that Divaker had already sacrificed many things to earn something on his own. He was neither doing any respectable job, nor was he earning well, but yes, he was doing something. That something was perhaps a lot of satisfaction for Maa. Divaker felt better after he hung up.

Divaker barely got time for studies. Half of his second year was gone, and he hardly ever looked into the pages of the study material. One Sunday he got up early and started studying. He realized how much time has gone by. When Gaurav woke up, he was surprised to see Divaker studying.

'It's good that you are turning pages now, half of the year is finished,' Gaurav said.

The very next day his second semester study material also arrived. Both the bundles put together occupied a full corner of their small room. The sight of those books gathering dust made him mad. He knew this was something he could not avoid. He had to start somewhere.

This was his sixth closing at Logos Finmart. After their training, it was only once that he had a chance to go to the bank. They had no reason of going to the bank; nobody at bank knew them. Harry was whole company for the boys, including Divaker. Harry paid their salary through demand draft, and gathered business from them. By the end of six months, half of their team members already left. He started doing well, month after month. He had a fairly good idea of what the bank people looked into an applicants documents. He did not waste time on parties whose case could never have been approved. Divakers hit-miss ratio was the best in his team, although he was not the best performer amongst them. Meanwhile, a fresh team of five boys joined Logos Finmart. Harry started spending more time with the new team, and Divaker spent more time in the field. Few of his old parties, gave references of their friends or family members willing to take a car loan. Business was smooth now, and he was doing ten to fifteen cases every month,

'I need twenty from you next month Divaker,' Harry said the other day.

'If everything goes on well, I will give you twenty five,' Divaker replied.

Harry was delighted. He wanted people like Divaker, to pull him up, and help him realize his dreams. Harry asked Divaker to induct a new boy into field one day. He was a fresh graduate

'You did not try any competitive exam or any other job?' Divaker asked the new boy once they were in field.

'Yes, I appeared for medical entrance exam twice after high school. After graduation, I also appeared for banking P.O entrance, but could not clear. Getting a job has become real tough. Dental and Medical colleges in Bangalore are asking something in between ten to fifteen lac rupees per seat. With that much money, its better to start your own business rather then waste five years doing a medical course. Above all, we do not have that much money,' the new boy said with an expression of irony and humor in his face.

'Yes, that's true buddy,' Divaker said.

In the evening, when Divaker felt that the boy had seen enough of job profile, they took a cold drink break, before leaving field for the day.

'How do you feel?' Divaker asked a broad question.

'It's like a salesman job. Isn't it?' the new boy asked back.

He was right, but somehow wrong too.

'It's not like a salesman job dear, it is a salesman job.' Divaker put emphasis on each word and corrected him. After a pause, he continued,' See everyone in this world is a salesman. Someone sells car finance schemes, someone sells detergents, and a shop owner is selling goods in his shop. A doctor is selling his services. It is true for a lawyer, an accountant, a roadside mechanic, everyone. Even a salaried teacher is selling his services,' Divaker pointed to a Maruti showroom opposite the road, 'You know? The owner of this showroom is a millionaire. What does he sell? Cars. Everyone has to sell something to earn something. This is a basic economic law and we all follow.'

'What time do I come tomorrow?' the boy asked.

'No need to meet me tomorrow. Your one-day induction is over. Meet Harry at nine o' clock in the office.'

The new boy joined, and in the first month gave good business. Divaker got an increment of five hundred rupees the same month. He had to compensate for his lack of scooter by putting in around two hours additional everyday.

'I would never be able to buy a scooter if I don't get ten thousand rupees from anywhere all of a sudden,' Divaker laughed and said to Gaurav one day.

'Things just don't happen out of the blue. Wait and watch. God sees everything and everything takes time. If your intentions are correct and efforts honest, you get what you want. As you say, it's only a matter of time,' they looked at each other. It was Gaurav who said this, and Divaker did not expect this piece to come from him.

Gaurav took out a cell phone from his pocket and showed it to him.

'I bought it today,' he said.

'Don't joke, must be someone's, and maybe you got a chance to hold it for a day or so. Isn't it?' Divaker did not believe.

Those days, cell phones were not seen in everyone's hand. For quite some time it was a rich man's possession, like a car and a big house. It was a lifestyle and luxury item. Today everyone in Divaker's family has a cell phone. He has two, but today's scenario was unimaginable that time. So, it was obvious for him to be surprised.

'Ok, don't believe. This is Nokia 5110 with an Airtel connection,' he opened up the battery and showed him the simcard.

'New?' Divaker asked.

'No, second hand. I met a person in Preet Vihar gift gallery. He wanted to sell his handset, and buy a new one.

'How much?' Divaker now started to believe.

'He was asking five thousand. I managed to get it for four. I knew the shopkeeper. I bought the simcard on credit from him.'

'You bought this stuff, okay, fine, but maintaining and using it is going to ruin you.'

'Yes, I know that. Ten rupees outgoing, and five rupees incoming per minute. I will not be making calls. I bought this only to receive calls. I miss a lot of business because I am not directly available to my customers. Titu often forgets to pass off my messages, and most of the time it is intentional,' Gaurav said.

Divaker observed the cell phone for some time. Understood the way in which it works and rang up Papa's number, but disconnected before anyone could pick up the receiver. Human needs have a tendency to grow. The more one gets, the more one wants.

Season changed and winter arrived, the chilling winter of

northern India. Divaker had only three months for his second year exams, and he wasn't even half through the syllabus. Doing two things at the same time is almost impossible. Saying, 'I will work during the day, and study at night,' may sound impressive, but in reality, work drained out his energy in such a way that he had nothing left to study at night. It wasn't like reading a novel, for studies one needs to concentrate on the subject, and with job stress and tension in mind, he would often find himself studying, but nothing actually going in his head.

Doing graduation was the first thing in his mind, after all why was he doing all this. He knew that he won't be doing any higher studies, but then a graduate degree was a minimum qualification required to do anything. Papa was a University topper, for Masters in Botany. His son; not even a graduate, this thought was a nightmare for him. Often Divaker lost hope and thought that he won't be able to complete the course, but then something inside him always pushed him to carry on. Divaker knew that there is a life, distant from him – where people dine in expensive restaurants, use cell phones, shop at branded malls, travel by flight, go to exotic vacations, and stay in five star hotels. He was growing up and his dreams were becoming big too. He did not know the way to find his dreams, but he knew that it's very difficult for a high school pass to realize those dreams. A graduation degree will at least give him entry to the path that leads to his dreams, without that he could not even start, leave aside the journey.

He understood that working for 'the man behind the desk,' or Harry is going to take him nowhere. He was an employee of Logos Finmart, not the big multinational bank where he was interviewed. He will keep on working with Harry, for God knows how much time, Harry would pat his back, when he did well and screw him up when he could not.

'Where is a career?'

'What next after this job of sales executive?'

'Am I really growing in terms of skills and experience?

'Will I never become someone, whom boys call Sir?'

'Is five hundred rupees increment from time to time all that I want?'

'Will I ever realize my dreams with what I am doing and how I am doing right now?'

Divaker knew the answer of these questions, and the answer that he had was not at all encouraging.

He could not have even passed the second year exam, in the way his studies were going on.

'What if I am held up, and I have to repeat the whole year?'

It was a prick in his ass, and a horror to imagine. He could not even imagine the idea of adding up one more year to the already painful process. Moreover, he felt that Delhi is not the right place to live. Increasing traffic day-by-day, pollution, extreme climate, selfish and indifferent people, all this made him feel that for some time its okay, but for settling down, never. A lot of socio-cultural difference and lack of warm personal touch in contacts worsened it more.

Where are the lush green paddy fields?

Where is the road by the river and the farmer carrying jute on his cycle?

Where is the breeze that whispers?

Alas! The lush green paddy fields give nothing more than rice.

The next day he met Harry in his cabin. He was having tea. In these nine months of professional acquaintance, Divaker never saw that Harry had the courtesy to ask the other person in his cabin for a cup of tea.

'I am working on a case of Mercedes. This will be the first Merc case from my side to the bank,' Harry informed happily.

'I want to talk to you regarding something,' Divaker said.

'Regarding what?' he asked, paying full attention.

'I have decided to resign?'

'What?' he asked in a tone of disbelief. He regained almost immediately, 'why? I mean, any problem?'

'No, no problem at your end, but then I don't have enough time for studies, and exams is looming large in front of me. I only have three months in my hand. You can perhaps understand how much I could study during the whole year.' Divaker presented his case.

'I knew, this happens. This is the problem. When guys start producing silver, they leave. I train fresh boys like you, teach them in and out of the business, after some time they become productive, and then they leave when somebody else throws in few hundred more.' Harry said infuriated. He paused for some time, took some deep breaths and continued, 'I know you are not that type of a guy, but if the problem is what I said better stay here. I will increase your salary from next month.'

'I understand the problem Sir, but this is not my reason for leaving. I told you the reason. Even if you give me a thousand rupee increment, I can't stay,' he made it very clear this time, and Harry perhaps understood.

'How many cases you have in your hands now?' Harry asked.

'I am working on four, not mature enough.'

'Ok, please give me the details so that I can ask someone to follow them up.'

Divaker took out few visiting cards and a notebook from his folio and briefed Harry about each one of them.

'Thank you Divaker,' Harry said and shook hands with Divaker, 'It was nice working with you.'

'My pleasure Sir, I learnt a lot of things working here.'

Divaker got up from the chair, and was about to leave.

'Normally you need to give one month notice for resignation. If someone resigns immediately, one-month salary is deducted. We don't have any such clause, as we don't maintain employees provident fund account. This is for your information only,' Harry said smiling.

Indirectly he wanted to convey that, he was in no mood to settle his wages for the last week he worked.

'No problem Sir, I just got my salary a week back. It's only a matter of one week,' Divaker replied casually. He did not want to muddle up the water after he had bathed. Moreover he could do nothing even if he wanted.

Divaker started his studies with all his heart and soul. He was not enjoying it, but the nightmare and his dreams compelled him to keep on moving. He did not inform anyone at home about the recent developments. They knew that that Divaker was still doing a job in some good car finance company. They did not know his job profile, Logos Finmart and Harry. That much information was enough for them. Divaker could not convey them the entire scenario over phone, that too in a time when long distance calling was expensive. Moreover, he had to call up Papa and Maa separately and narrate the same story twice. He did not know exactly why, but yes, they were not aware of the detailed version of his story.

Divaker needed money. He had no savings, and he had to keep

going for the next three months anyhow, to study and pass the second year exams, to complete his graduation, to enter the next phase of life and to realize his dreams. He had no other option. He shamelessly called up Papa. By that time, Divaker knew this feeling called 'bitter acceptance.'

'This month or the next I need some money,' he said.

'But you are doing a job now. You are earning well,' Papa said in a panicky shaky voice.

'Yes, but I am in need.'

'What need? Is there any problem?' Papa asked, sensing something grossly wrong.

'No, nothing wrong, no need to worry, I am just running short of money.'

'I told you a hundred times not to overspend. If you are earning one and spending two, you will always run short of money.'

For a few seconds the thought of telling Papa everything came to his mind, but he did not want to prolong the discussion. It was difficult for people like Papa to understand that how easily he quit the job. For them, a job means lifetime security, as it used to happen in their times. Government sector jobs are vanishing day by day, hundreds of thousand candidates apply for a single vacancy. Selection is more of luck or internal arrangements, rather than talent. Everything is run by commerce, and people are getting used to this fact gradually.

'I did not overspend,' Divaker said, and listened quietly to the sermon that flowed from the other end of the receiver.

'Ok, how much? Papa asked, once he was through.

'Same, as you used to send every month.'

'Ok, I will arrange,' Papa said and hung up.

From that day onwards, Papa used to say the following verbatim to whosoever met him, at home, on the streets, in bank, in vegetable market, and in his office:

'Divaker is a nice boy, but he is a spendthrift fellow. Yes, he earns well, but spends more than what he earns. See, he is doing a job there, but where other kids send their parents money back home. I have to send him money even today.'

The listener would sympathize with Papa and he felt satisfied. The listener would then narrate Papa's woeful tale to few others as well. Misty told Divaker about this part years later.

One month went by with the last salary from Logos Finmart. In between, the money order also arrived. For the next two months, he studied and stayed indoors most of the time, going out for dinner or any other important reason only, as and when required.

'You are going to get scholarship this year,' Gaurav said, joking one day, while getting ready for work.

'No, I am preparing for Adminstrative Service Exams.'

They both laughed, and Divaker kicked him on his butt.

'No, but seriously, if you had put the same efforts for whole year, even if not the Administrative Services, you would have definitely been among the toppers in your University.'

'Joking again?' Divaker asked.

'No, serious, really,' Gaurav said seriously, 'Ok, bye, see you in the evening. He left the room with two big cartons of artificial flower bouquet.

Divaker had asked a newspaper vendor to drop by a copy everyday. As a break from his studies, he used to browse through it everyday. Payment was again on a fifty-fifty basis. Gaurav hardly ever read newspaper. Divaker never saw him reading. Yes, he used the old newspapers as packing material for his bouquets. On Wednesdays, a separate supplement with newspaper featured all sorts of job. The good companies advertised vacancies in that supplement. All types of job; finance, HR, Sales and Marketing, Software, Technical, Non-technical etc..etc... were featured in that supplement. Any readable piece of paper can always give some information. His understanding and knowledge about the 'job world' was increasing. There are few companies, which pay well, they are called 'good paymasters', and most of them are multinational companies. Some of the Indian companies also pay handsomely. All of them have varied needs:

B.Tech or diploma in Electrical Engg.

B.Tech with M.B.A.

M.B.A with experience.

M.Tech in Biotechnology.

M.B.B.S from a govt medical college.

M.B.A with proficiency in computers.

These were not the only vacancies released. He found himself fit to apply for some others like:

Graduates with fluency in English, two years experience.

Graduates in any stream, one to three year experience.

However, not now, maybe after one year, when he is through with the Graduation, he can apply. This world is huge. There are different people, different qualifications, different jobs and yes, different salary packages.

The more sugar you add, the more sweet your tea is.

From three months, now his exams were only three days away. His first exam was for accountancy. The examinations were spread out with few days in between.

In a month, all the exams were over. He was now free again. Still a month, or more, for the results to roll out. This was the time he enjoyed most. No study material lying in the corner of the room, no job, no tension.

5

Destiny's Conspiracy

One day, Gaurav brought a visitor to the room and introduced him.

'This is Arman; he was a regular customer at Titu's shop. We became friends, but after leaving Titu's shop, I was not much in contact with him,' Gaurav said.

Arman was a well-built tall guy. He was fair, and had long fashionable hair. Also, his clothes were in tune with the latest fashion, and he wore a pair of Ray-Ban glasses.

'It's a fortunate chance that I met Gaurav at a gift shop in Connaught Place today. He insisted and so I came down to see where he is putting up,' Arman said.

Gaurav introduced Divaker, and soon they started talking on things not relevant to either one of them – weather, movies, cellular operators, etc. Arman loved showing off an expensive cell phone handset. He was continuously playing with it, while talking to Divaker. Gaurav brought few coke bottles from the store downstairs. Divaker learnt for the conversation that Arman had a leather product business in Gali Nabi Kareem, Paharganj. Arman stayed for half an hour and then left saying that, he has to attend business. Gaurav and Divaker, both went downstairs to see him going. He drove off in a white Maruti 800. Gaurav was smiling when he came back to the room.

'What happened?' Divaker asked.

'Nothing, I was just wondering how far one's destiny can take.'

'Why?'

'This fellow, Arman is a bloody big fucker,' he laughed,

'Like you?'

'No, he is greater than me. I am just a novice, and I learnt all about this from him only.'

'Oh, I see. He must be a rich kid then. Lot of money to spend and afford the lifestyle he leads.'

'Bullshit rich kid! His elder brother does it all. I know his brother very well. He wears a lungi and a vest throughout the year and makes shoes and wallet in Nabi Kareem. By the time Arman joined, they already had their own small shop there. Arman's elder brother asked him to come and work when he failed to pass the matriculation exam two consecutive years. His brother developed all the customer and parties; he gave supplies to Titu's shop also. Sale picked up soon from their small shop, and a year back they bought a bigger shop in Paharganj. Now Arman does nothing, but sits there whole day counting cash.'

'Ok, hmmm......'

'When you have nothing in your head, you follow your instincts. First hunger, if it is taken care of, then sex.'

Although Gaurav was not well educated, his basic fundamentals in life were clear. Some day; the same week, Gaurav was going to meet Arman at his shop in Paharganj. He asked Divaker to accompany him, and he agreed.

Their shop was actually two small shops put together. One

portion was used as storeroom, and the other portion was shop or office – whatever they called. It had a small one-ton window air-conditioner installed at the floor level to save space, which did not cool even the face of the person sitting in front of it. He welcomed us like a mock king, and we were messengers from a distant kingdom.

'Tea, coffee or something cold,' he asked.

'It's already so hot, we will have some cold drink,' Gaurav said. Arman asked a boy of ten or twelve years working in his shop to fetch some bottles. Divaker recognized his elder brother counting and labeling some leather wallets. Nobody felt the need of introducing him, or asking him for a cold drink.

'Next Sunday come at Hotel Satkar,' Arman said.

'Hotel Satkar, Karolbagh?' Gaurav asked.

'Yes, same.'

'What for?'

'It's my birthday..........,' he could not complete.

'........and you are going to give us a party, right?' Gaurav completed the sentence.

'Umm.. Not exactly. It's Deepika who is giving a party.'

Later, Divaker came to know from Gaurav, that Deepika is Arman's girlfriend with whom he was going straight for the last one year.

'But you said that he needs a fresh face every month,' Divaker asked.

'Yes, that's true. That has taken a backseat these days. If somebody comes in, fine, he will not turn his face off and please the girl, but this affair is serious. I met Deepika twice. She is not as pretty as you might be thinking, but yes, she is very caring and friendly. Arman knows that he won't find a girl like her to marry, it's better not to lose such a person, and you know how sweet spoken he is.'

'Yeah, that's true,' Divaker agreed.

Gaurav was right. Deepika was a soft spoken and very well behaved girl. She cordially talked to them, when they reached Hotel Satkar next Sunday. She had a graceful aura around her, and nothing about her was cheap. Divaker could not talk to her much as she was busy with other guests and the arrangements, but Divaker gathered with whatever little talk he had with her that, she was utterly caring, and she understood feelings and emotions very well. She was doing a bachelor degree course in dental science from a respectable government medical college.

What a combination! The boy a non metric thickhead and the girl a doctor........

Deepika introduced Divaker to her younger sister, Prerna. Arman and Deepika knew most of the people, and all of them were strangers to Divaker. Prerna was sitting at a table near Divaker. They started talking, and for rest of the evening they kept on talking. Gaurav kept on wagging his tail here and there, meeting new people, making more contacts, and trying to impress everyone with his sweet urdu mixed language, that he had learnt from Arman.

Divaker had a nice time talking to Prerna. For the first time in his life, he had such a long chat with a stranger of the opposite gender. He felt nice. She gave her phone number to Divaker and asked him to call up.

'I shall wait for your call,' she said again, when Gaurav and Divaker started their scooter. The party was over, and a sweet flavor lingered in Divaker's mind.

'You had a nice time, huh?' Gaurav asked.

'Yes, but she is not like her sister Deepika.' Divaker replied.

'Why?'

'She is a bit immature and impulsive. She does not have the mental depth............,' Divaker could not complete.

'Who asked you to measure mental depth stupid? Look out for some other depths and enjoy life buddy,' Gaurav interrupted and started laughing hysterically.

Divaker looked away at other direction pretending he did not hear anything.

They were already full from the party, so just after changing clothes they rolled on the mattress, talking about the party, Deepika, Arman, food, other people, and Prerna.

'But one thing I tell you,' Gaurav continued, that girl is interested in you.'

'How do you know?'

'I have seen enough of these things. If somebody senior is saying something, it is out of his experience and exposure, so better believe and trust him.'

'Ok, maybe.'

Divaker knew that Prerna was interested in him but he did not want to accept it. He wanted to, but he could not. Something was stopping him to believe it. It was as if a child says,

'Don't wake me up Mama; I am seeing a beautiful fairy dream.'

Next day Divaker called her from a public phone booth.

'I knew you will call up,' she said.

'I called up because I knew you were waiting.'

She giggled.

Gaurav returned in the evening that day, frustrated, depressed and irritated.

'I need to buy a car,' he announced as soon as he entered.

'Everything fine,' Divaker enquired.

'The goods are all damaged today. The packet at my back hit a car at the traffic red light. All the materials spread on the road, to be crushed by speeding cars. I could do nothing except watch.'

Divaker knew that it had to happen sooner or later. Whenever he saw him tying those big cartons sometime at the back of scooter, sometime in front, Divaker wondered how he manages to ride. But no, nothing seemed to bother Gaurav. He would kick start the small vehicle, squeeze himself on the seat and off he went, with the cartons dangling, hanging and shaking. Divaker wanted to help him. He felt very bad for the humiliation and loss that Gaurav incurred.

'How much can you pay right now,' Divaker asked him.

'I don't have much, only five six thousand.'

'With five-six thousand rupees you cannot even get a scooter. I will try to get a loan for you but then you will have to manage the down payment, registration, insurance etc, which all put together will be around thirty thousand.'

'Thirty thousand?' Gaurav was surprised.

'Yes, thirty thousand, this too in a rare case of ninety percent finance, which the bank does not prefer generally.'

'I will try. A lot of money is rolled up in business as credit given to local shops.'

'How much is that amount?' Divaker asked.

'Around fifty thousand. If I follow up, request them to pay a bit early and tell them my problem. I think they will understand. Most of them are at good terms with me. If not more I can gather ten to fifteen thousand.'

'Good enough. Plus, if you sell off your old scooter, how much more money will come?' Divaker asked.

'Nobody will give anything more than five or six thousand for this old trash can.'

'Another five thousand, that adds up to twenty thousand,' Divaker said to Gaurav in an encouraging tone.

Gaurav was relaxed now. He was smiling. Perhaps he could see the silver lining.

'It means another ten thousand, and I own a car?' Gaurav asked.

'Yes, almost, but there are other things you need to do,' Divaker said.

'Like?'

'You have a bank account?'

'Yes.'

'How old is that?'

'Three years, almost.'

'Any cheque bounces in the last six months?'

'None, hardly ever used a cheque, most of the work in cash only.'

'Ok, fine. Can you manage a residential proof like electricity bill or telephone bill?' Divaker asked.

They decided to take a phone connection. Divaker agreed to pay half of the connection and installation cost – fifty fifty rule – but only after he had some cash with him.

The landline phone was installed in their room within a week. Now, it was easy for Divaker to talk with Prerna. Once they ended up talking for hours together, and then, very often they used to talk for hours. It was time for the first and last date in Diavker's life.

'Can we meet? It's been a long that we met last time.' Divaker urged.

She agreed, and one fine morning they met at Dilli Haat. It was a theme village type of a place, with stalls selling handicrafts, woodwork, terracotta, and similar kind of stuff from all across India.

She gave him a beautiful card that day. The card is still with Divaker even today. He doesn't know exactly where, Devyani must have kept it somewhere, but yes, it's still with him.

He read the card, and said, 'I don't believe much in a friendship kind of a relationship Prerna.'

'Why?' she asked softly, and looked directly into Divaker's dreamy eyes.

'I believe in relationships that are more stable, secure and long lasting. Tomorrow we both will get married to some different persons, and our so-called friendship will end. In our society no matter how liberal we call ourselves, but then something bothers us if our spouse has a friend of opposite sex,' Divaker clarified.

'But then, nobody knows how far a relationship might go. If we start today as friends, maybe tomorrow we may give a new definition to our relationship, who knows. Isn't it?'

She was right. Even Divaker was also right, but to an extent, and Gaurav was completely right when he said that Divaker was a stupid.

Divaker told her that he would be interested only if she commits to a lifelong relationship, and that he has nothing in his hands as of now, but only God knows what tomorrow has in store for him. Divaker said that nobody in his family has ever owned a car, and he has a tractor and a bullock cart back in his distant village; where the world ends, and lush green paddy fields extend to as far as one can see. He told her every possible bull shit that a girl maybe least interested in hearing on a date.

Lastly, he conveyed the core feeling of his heart, in the most sensitive possible way; holding her hands and looking deep inside her dark eyelashes and bright eyes –

'I love you Prerna, and I would like to have you as my companion for lifetime. I want to marry you in future.'

Prerna asked for some time to think over it, and Divaker agreed.

Next day his second year results were out and he scored 63.2 percent aggregate. It was an insignificant three percent increase over last year. The result was better than his expectation, and he was honestly happy about it. Studies, result, job and every other thing important to him some time back, had suddenly taken a backseat for the last month and a half. Yes, all this happened fast, and all this happened in less then two months.

He waited for two full days and nights for her call. She did not call up, Divaker called her at the end of second day.

'Hello, yes,' she said in a sleepy voice.

'Are you alright? It seems as if you are not well.'

'No, nothing, just maybe flu or something. How are you?'

'I had been waiting for your call.'

'Oh, yes. See Divaker, I don't think its going to work out the way you want. Firstly, my parents are not going to agree to our inter-caste marriage. Secondly, without knowing each other well, I don't think we are in a position to commit something to each other.'

She had no idea, that Divaker did not want her commitment, but an emotional security, which he had been deprived off, since childhood. For Divaker, one and a half month was enough to know and understand her, but as Gaurav said once:

"If you want to understand and know someone; you will understand the person in few days, and if you don't want; even a lifetime will be short."

Maybe Prerna was at the other angle of observing the same thing. He kept on saying to himself:

Neither of us is wrong.

Neither of us is wrong.

Neither of us is wrong.

Neither of us is wrong.

Whatever it was, till day he could not understand what possibly went wrong that day or the series of events that happened after they met in Dilli Haat. Few irritating questions kept on bothering him –

Why did she react in that way?

Why was I over expecting and demanding in my attitude?

Why is it that marriage was at the top of my mind when I just got a chance to know a girl of my age?

Has my past programmed me to think in terms of mistrust and insecurity?

He could not find answers to these questions. Their relationship ended, before it could even start. Divaker did not blame her, because he knew, that he himself was also wrong in quite some ways, and he had nothing to offer at that time. Long time back, Divaker had read a book by Paulo Coelho and remembered something called 'Destiny's Conspiracy.' He was not shattered or disappointed over the matter, but yes, his experience kept him wondering, and thinking.

6

The Small Town

This was his last year in Delhi. He took admission for the third year course and the study material arrived. There was time in his hand, and he was running short of money. The job supplement helped him. Divaker got a job in a good Pharma company as Medical Representative. This was an Indian company, called Acos Laboratories, with turnover worth thousand million rupees per annum.

They had asked for graduates, but Divaker was so confident with his previous selections that he decided to try his luck. After all, what could be the worst-case scenario? He asked himself and decided to appear for the interview.

'Will you be able to sell medicines? It requires technical knowledge of the products, and the way they work,' they had asked him.

'Yes Sir, sure. I have sold floor cleaners and luxury cars. I can sell medicines also. Technical knowledge I will acquire,' he had replied confidently.

'You have one year to complete your graduation. Until that time, you will be a trainee. Moreover, we have a standard probationary period of nine months as company policy,' they informed him, and the same day he got his appointment letter.

It read - :

To,

Mr. Divaker Acharya,

SUB – Appointment as Trainee Medical Representative.

He was selected in a batch of ten boys and two girls. They all had had classroom training for two weeks. They were taught everything relevant to the trade like – Human Physiology, Etiology of disease, pharmacokinetics and Pharmacodynamics of the drugs etc etc. He did well in the tests conducted after trainings. On the last day, they were put into a division selling antibiotics and painkillers.

His job started. It was like meeting ten doctors and three retailers everyday and detailing them about the product portfolio. He soon learned that how does the market behave, what was his role, and how to fight market competition.

Acos Laboratories was a professionally managed company. He got salary slips every month, with classification of Basic Pay; House rent allowance, PF deduction etc. It turned out around four thousand rupees per month, plus daily allowance of seventy-five rupees. Monetarily, Divaker was not benefited much as compared to his job at Logos Finmart, but here he saw a career. Divaker reported to Mr. Massey, who was his supervisor. Mr. Massey reported to Mr. Dhawan (Regional Manager). Mr. Dhawan reported to Mr. Bahl (Zonal Manager), and Mr.Bahl reported to Sanjiv Taneja – General Manager. Divaker was at the grass root level but; he could see the whole tree, standing upright in front of him.

Divaker felt great to see his name in print, on visiting cards.

He was a full time employee of a big organization. Festival bonus, medical reimbursement, LTA, etc – he saw and learned new things. Every month they had a meeting to discuss about last month performance and plan for the new. He was not a fast learner, but later he did very well and earned incentives for two month in a row.

Once they had a half-yearly conference at The Taj Hotel, Maan Singh Road – a respectable five star property in the heart of city. He did not say to anyone, that it was for the first time he ever entered the gates of such a grand place.

The phone in their room was quite old now, and the bills used to come every two months. But, the bills could never be used for the purpose it was planned. The silver lining vanished very soon from Gaurav's horizon. Maybe he had lost hopes, and left everything for destiny to decide, just like Divaker. Gaurav was working hard, and Divaker as a friend could feel it. He knew that one day Gaurav would achieve and realize his dreams.

Acos Laboratories was a big company for Divaker, very big, with employees posted in every part of the country. They had a manufacturing plant in Bangalore, and portfolio of more than fifty brands put together. They were into almost everything – ophthalmology, neurology, cardiology, diabetes care, dermatology etc.. etc. Hundreds of people working throughout the country, he felt good to be a part of this big company. That time, he had little idea about companies in which people work in every part of the globe.

He told about this career move to Papa over phone.

Divaker worked for full one year with Acos Laboratories. The job was tough. For every product they had, the market was already full with two dozen different brands. Acos Laboratories was one of those two dozen companies. He came to know that there is something called 'Patent', which we do not have in our country. Introduction of Patent would have threatened Acos Lab, as well as Divaker's job. Acos Lab had no R&D; it was a company like most of Indian Pharma companies, which copied drugs from west, and manufactured them locally at fraction of cost. There was nothing major to differentiate them from the rest of the competition. Acos Lab was huge for Divaker, but soon he realized that there are bigger fishes in the pond, much bigger. In sales – as in other walks of life – the basic things are same. He was responsible to meet a monthly sales target. In his case it was one hundred fifty thousand to begin with, and it gradually increased to two hundred thousand rupees per month. Every month they had to close their sales by month end. Detergents and floor cleaners, then car finance schemes, and then pharmaceuticals. He felt as if he had come up a long way, but still it was a long walk ahead.

Divaker was given confirmation letter on time, at the end of nine months probation period. Nobody ever asked about the graduation issue. They did not wait for it, and he was confirmed with the remaining four surviving batch mates. From time to time in that one-year period, he heard that somebody resigned or somebody was asked to resign. They were reduced to only four, from a team of twelve. He saw the coming of three such teams during his stay at Acos. People come and go, some stay longer. Nobody bothers; life goes on.

Just one month after his confirmation and two months before the exams, he resigned from Acos. He had few very valuable things with him now; his appointment letter, confirmation letter and salary slips. He knew it was enough to prove his experience with a good and average pharma company. Once you have a little work experience in this trade, you don't have difficulty finding a new employer. The companies also get a new employee in a day's time. Millions of educated unemployed had to go somewhere. There are people Divaker knew, who are willing to work for free.

Divaker had other priorities to face – the final year exams. The sequencing of events was similar for all the three years in Delhi.

Job – studies – exams – job – studies – exams ....

He was bored of life and the monotony. He kept wondering that how other like his maternal uncle kept on doing the same thing for years and years.

Breakfast – local bus – office – lunch – local bus – one room apartment – dinner – sleep – breakfast – local bus ....

Divaker wanted to escape everything. After the final year exams he rushed back to meet his people at home. It was a comeback after two long years, and after two days of long journey by train and bus. He felt that he had grown up a lot during those two years. Somewhere down the way, he had lost his childhood innocence and spontaneous energy of youth. He was a weary man, with invisible wrinkles on face. He wanted to relax and sleep, as if he hasn't slept for months.

When Divaker left Delhi, he did not tell Gaurav that his chances of coming back were almost nil, he could not come to terms with the reality that he was going to lose such a friend forever. Divaker did not know where and why he was heading. He just wanted to escape from the grind. He had no place to go except the rented house where Papa and Misty stayed in a remote town of Assam, and Maa, four hundred miles away in an unknown village of West Bengal – where the world ends, and lush green paddy fields cover the earth to as far as one can see.

Divaker did not inform them in advance about his arrival. It was all of a sudden that he appeared. They knew that his exams were over, and he could come any day. Rainy season in Assan lasts pretty long as compared to rest of the country. It rains for almost half of the year. The rickshawalla wrapped in a polythene sheet – serving the purpose of raincoat – pulled Divaker slowly over the bumpy, water filled potholes of the road. It was a small town, sparsely populated, with a forest and two rivers in the vicinity. In ten minutes from the bus stop, Divaker was in front of the house.

Papa opened the door and Misty hugged Divaker.

'Come, come, sit down. Torrential rains here for the last three days. It stopped this morning only. How was your journey?' Papa asked.

'Journey was kind of good. Its hot there in Delhi, here at least the rains have kept down the heat,' Divaker said.

'And what about your exams?' Papa asked.

'I did well, lets see. Results will be coming bv next month end.'

'That's great! two months! two months! you will be staying for two months. That's sooooo……. Nice,' Misty was overwhelmed with joy.

'Not too much luggage?' Papa observed.

Papa perhaps expected Divaker to arrive with all the bag and baggage, which included a bedroll, pillow, quilt and a large suitcase or trunk. Divaker did not ever want to travel with lots of baggage. It was always easy traveling light. Moreover, he did not buy any of those things while he was in Delhi. Divaker does not remember precisely from where all those stuff came. The mattress was lying in the room before he started living in it, and maybe, perhaps the quilt, pillow etc found their way with Gaurav. He went there with a bag and came back with a bag. That's all.

It was late afternoon and Divaker was having tea with them.

The dog sat near him wagging tail. The dog actually had a name – Moti. Misty brought Moti as a month year old puppy, one day while returning from school. He had fallen in a muddy ditch, and was shivering. Since that day, Moti had been a part of their family.

'It's alright, but you quit your job, and that's what troubling me,' Papa said with an expression of hopelessness and failure, without looking at Divaker.

Divaker said nothing and wondered what Papa expected him to do àfter three long years of stay in Delhi, and having written the final year grads exam.

'I have plans, once my results are out, I have some plans,' Divaker said, although he wasn't sure of any such plan.

The grotesque expression on Papa's face thickened.

'In all these years you have not been able to buy a mattress or a quilt or even a pillow. At least that's what I understand, from the way you came; empty handed. I doubt whether you have really appeared for the final year exams or not,' having said this, Papa felt relieved as if a burden has been taken off his head.

Misty heard everything, understood, and got annoyed. Afterwards, she pretended to hear nothing, and continued talking to their dog. The dog wagged his tail and sniffed. It was humid, rains had stopped, and sharp sunlight made the water soaked earth puff out steam. Divaker asked Misty to come for a walk down the small river that flowed two hundred yards away from their backyard. The river was overflowing and few fishermen in small boats were pulling out their nets from water.

'So, by next week your exams will be over too?' Divaker asked her.

'Yes, only social science left.'

'I am planning to visit Maa next week,' he said.

They were walking by the river and the river flowed with speed he never saw before. The river flowed smoothly, but he could feel its speed by the debris it carried along. Misty was silent for some time. Their dog saw something in the hedge and started barking.

'I will be going along with you. Is it okay?' she asked.

'Well fine, no problem. Talk to Papa about it.'

They could not visit Maa without taking permission from Papa.

Rest of the evening Divaker watched TV, and Misty studied. Papa made dinner. By the time they could finish the dinner, it started raining again; and a power-cut made things worse.

'It happens here, almost everyday, six hours or so,' Papa said.

'There is no use waiting, where are the candles?' Divaker asked. They had a forced candle light dinner.

Divaker heard frogs croaking at a distance, and occasional howling of foxes. Lying on bed in the darkness, he thought how different and varied human life is. There in Delhi, all night he heard traffic noise coming from the window that looked down on the street below. He suddenly felt as if he is alone in this big-big world. He felt happy for some time, visualizing the benefits, a moment later he was horrified. He started thinking something else. A streak of candlelight was entering from the other room where Misty was studying, and he realized that he was not alone.

'Put out the candle and sleep early. Don't stress your eyes and mind. Better study tomorrow,' Divaker said.

'Hmmm... ten more minutes Bhai.'

He must have slept soon. In his dreams he saw the 'man behind the desk' stroking and bumping over the cheaply dressed receptionist – both naked. They saw him, and gave a malicious smile. He saw the overflowing river and fishermen on their tiny boats. He saw the dog running towards him, panting with his tongue hanging out in air, but no matter how fast he ran, he could never reach him.

The morning was bright when Divaker woke up. The rain had flushed all the dullness and crisp clear sunlight fell upon every wet blade of grass. It took him few seconds to realize why Gaurav was not there, why their small room in Delhi looked big, and from where the TV came. He was at Papa's place in Assam. It was eight o' clock, but it seemed that more of the morning had already passed. There in Delhi, morning begins at eight o'clock. Bangladesh on the same longitude of Assam has a different time zone – half an hour reduced. A single standard time is followed throughout the nation, but if observed carefully the time gap is apparent.

Tea and breakfast all made and served by Papa, toast, half-fried eggs and a glass of carrot juice. When was the last time Divaker had a proper breakfast.........Anyway, it was a real treat. Papa stayed at home most of the time. He was both father and mother for Misty. He had nothing significant to do. The public sector warehousing company he worked for was under scrutiny by 'Board of Investigation for Sick Industries.' The government made companies, gave jobs to people, but corruption and mismanagement brought these companies at the verge of closure. The employees were now a sore throat to the government and to the bleeding financial resources.

They were almost a dozen office bearers, including Papa, in that small town, who had nothing to do except sip tea in the office verandah, and chat about the developments happenings at supreme court regarding the case and fate of their organization. Papa stayed home almost all day. He cooked, took care of Misty and he did the entire housekeeping job. Misty was used to this arrangement but Divaker never felt comfortable because things were not this way before.

Divaker stayed there for a week. Misty was through with her exams, and so they started off to meet Maa one morning.

Two hours of journey by bus, to the nearest railway station, eight hours of journey by train, an hour in bus again and half an hour on foot. They reached the village where the world ends, lush green paddy fields, small rivers and ponds everywhere. Their family had some respect in the village. Everyone thought that Papa was in a great job, and the kids are being educated to the best possible extent. In short, Divakers family was role model for everyone. For a few days people flocked to meet them, most of the people never known to Divaker. Maa also took them to dozens of her friends and relatives place in that small village, and they marched like a pair of grizzlies, catching everyone's attention. It was not possible to interpret what everyone said, but whatever they said was a mix of admiration or astonishment.

Divaker heard things like –

'You got a job in a bank?'

'How much salary?'

'Like father, like son,'

'This kid grew up as if he is fed on urea. One day he will be bigger man than his father.'

'You will take Maa to live with you. Isn't it?'

Divaker would grin, smile and say –

'Yes.'

'Ummm......'

'Sure'

They stayed there for a week and then started their way back to the small town in Assam, where Papa lived. Half of the village came to see them off. Maa wept, Misty wept, and so did few other women, whom he did not know precisely. They sat on a riksha with a suitcase and bag. The rickshawallah pulled by hand as the brick leveled road made it impossible for him to paddle. Slowly and slowly, they went past the small river, paddy fields, bamboo thickets, and after almost an hour they reached the pukka road. They traveled overnight by train and the next morning reached Papa's place.

In small towns, and small peoples life, nothing significant happens. It was the same routine almost everyday.

Breakfast – do nothings – bath – lunch – afternoon sleep – tea – do nothing – dinner – bed time – breakfast – do nothings – bath – lunch...............

The 'do nothings' were mostly watching TV, playing with the dog or videogame. Often Divaker accompanied Papa to the vegetable market on the old motorcycle – the registration number turned out thirteen – the motorcycle was not very old those days. He also helped Papa in the kitchen.

A week went by and then a month. Divaker called up Gaurav one day to get some information about the University results. Gaurav called him back the next day and said that the results are out. Divaker gave his roll number and asked him to get details of marks. Those days results were not available on the internet. Things are a lot easier these days. The mark sheet in original could be obtained only in person. Gaurav again called up the next day, and informed him that he had passed the final year graduation exam with second division, 58.2 percent to be precise. Divaker missed the first division grade by 1.8 percent.

'What happened?' Papa asked, as Divaker hung up the phone.

'I have passed.'

'How much?'

'Sixty percent,' Divaker said with an expressionless face.

'Good, but these days nothing significant happens with a mere first division. You know, your Sahu uncle's son. He passed with a distinction two years back, seventy eight percent. Doing nothing these days. No job, nothing,' Papa had briefed him enough about a future possibility.

Divaker did not talk to him for the rest of the day. Firstly, he felt guilty for concealing the truth about his result, and secondly he felt alone and helpless in this big-big world. The person called 'Papa' did nothing but made a mockery of his failures. Divaker knew that he did not have a fall back cushion. Divaker thought about the prospect of telling him that, he did not even secure a first division grade, missed it by 1.8 percent, and imagined his reaction. He smiled, and kept quite.

It had become apparent that he had to do something very soon, something for his career and future. Things could not go on like this forever – 'doing nothings.' But he did not know what to do. Divaker had a vague blueprint, but nothing consolidated. He had no idea from where to start. He had his dreams on a far horizon, standing tall like a mountain, but he did not know the path that would take him there. His instincts told him to start the journey, and that he would find a path. Divaker believed in God and his instincts. This faith and the need gained urgency and momentum when one evening they were having tea, and the dog was going round and round a bush.

'Now what? What do you plan to do next?' Papa asked.

Divaker did not have specific answer to this question. He wanted to do MBA from a good institute, but he also knew that there is a wide gap between desire and reality. A gap that could be bridged only with resources; and resources means money. This gap had always divided the 'have' and 'have not'. In his case, he did not have the resources. Papa perhaps understood what he was thinking.

'These days it takes hundred thousands rupees to study courses like engineering, medical and even MBA. We are a middle-income group family and thinking on those lines means wastage of time. Had you been an extraordinary student, you could have easily got scholarship or some grant. I am an average earning man. As a father, I would always like to see my son studying at the best colleges, but there are limitations to things. If you wish to study further, you can take admission for master's course at the P.L.Barua College. One of my colleague's son goes there, he is doing his graduation. You can study from home. But, I feel that the 'home factor' should not come in between you and your career. In case of latter, I would never stop you to take your own course of action. You may go anywhere; Delhi, Bombay, Kolkata, anywhere, but you will have to be on your own, as my support has a limitation. Otherwise, what happened to the company you had been working? Will they take you back?' Papa finished delivering his message.

By the time Papa finished, many of Divaker's doubts were already resolved, and he chalked out a plan for things to come.

He made a hand written resume and got it typed at an electronic typewriter shop near civil court. He looked at it, and felt that it had some weight now. A weight gained with three years of sweat, sun and toil. He started applying for jobs, first by couriers, then by ordinary post.

'These courier people take a lot of money, fifteen rupees per envelope to Kolkata. The same thing can be done in three rupees also,' Papa said one day. There was no use making him understand that by courier, the document reaches next day, and there is a proof of delivery. The same thing by ordinary post takes a week, and no proof of delivery.

Divaker had applied for close to thirty jobs and was called for two interviews, but he was not selected. They mostly conducted their interviews in Kolkata, which was the nearest metro city of that region.

Lastly, a company called up to appear in its selection process, two rounds of group discussion, written test, and then two interviews. Out of eight hundred people, only four were selected. It was a big multinational company. Divaker had to report to their Delhi office for training. They did not say anything about the place of posting. It would be decided only after completion of twenty-one day classroom training.

Divaker felt that this was a good company to work. They had a legacy of more than hundred years, a global operation in around one hundred twenty five countries, and a fortune 500 ranking. It was a pharmaceutical company with lot of investment into Research and Development. Apart from this, he felt good about this company from the way people interacted, their systems and processes. He looked back and thought that things just kept on getting better. They were going to pay a base salary of six thousand rupees, plus allowances every month. It was more than enough for him that time; in fact, it was a handsome package to begin with. Papa told this news to all his friends along with the salary package.

Within a week, he had to start for Delhi.

'Better if they give you a posting in West Bengal or Assam,' Papa said, when Divaker was about to leave.

'Yes, let's see.'

What if they send you to a far off place like Bangalore or

Hyderabad or Bombay?' Misty asked, the corner of her eyes were moist. In spite of entering initial teen years, she was still a child at heart.

'No, that wont be,' Divaker said, concealing his thoughts.

Moti wagged his tail understanding something, Perhaps nothing.

7

The New Life

Divaker completed the three-week classroom training in Delhi. The company was expanding and they had recruited close to forty people all over the country. Everyday from morning nine to evening six, they were run through presentations and the next day tests were conducted. Divaker performed above average in all the tests. He had a chance to mix with people across the country – Chennai, Ahmedabad, Nagercoil, Jaipur, Bhubaneshwar, Jammu, Trichur, etc, etc. On weekends, they used to take them to movie shows or restaurants.. It was a damn good experience but then everyone was concerned about the place of posting, just like him.

It was their last evening at the Guest House cum training centre. The company had thrown in a party with fabulous food and entertainment. The training manager mounted a small stage, and everyone's eyes followed.

'Okay! friends, its time to announce your place of posting, something you all had been looking forward to anxiously for the last three weeks. Let me take you through the process. Each candidate is presented in front of a committee, which decides the initial place of posting for each one of you. It's a mix of your skill areas, talent, territorial profile and company's requirements. So, please don't be disheartened if you don't get a posting of your choice. I assure you that whatever has been decided is in the best interest of your career, and your own development. Best of luck to each one of you,' he said.

A pin drop silence prevailed throughout the hall where they had assembled. Suddenly all the hype and hoopla vanished, they watched each others face. It was like a TV game show – suspense and excitement. The training manager started calling names followed by the place of posting, followed by a round of forced applause from the crowd. The applause ended before gaining pitch as everyone thought that the next name would be his or her. Divaker's heart was racing and palms sweating. Where could it be???

Calcutta – Good! Somewhere near my family.

Chennai – Not so good! Too far off.

Delhi – Never! Never!

Bombay – Where will I be putting up?

Nellore – I don't know where it is.

Suddenly.........

'Divaker Acharya, our Trainee Territory Manager, to be based at Meerut, U.P!' the training Manager announced. A round of applause; even Divaker clapped, but he now heard the voices from a far off place, faintly. He was in a mixed emotion mode. He did not know, whether he should be happy or disheartened or disappointed. The programme was over soon, and everybody joined in for dinner.

'It's a good place to begin your career, a very potential territory,' the training manager said, putting a piece of cucumber in his mouth.

'Once we did very well in Meerut, our guy over there won all India topper award two years back,' a senior personnel voluntarily waded near him with a plate full of curry.

'Oh! Is it? Nice for me,' Divaker wore a compulsive smile and said.

'Very potential belt, lots of diabetics over there, and good affordability. Even the farmers earn a lot. They grow sugarcane and feed the mills in and around. Just sow and harvest stuff...... Not the farmers, I mean. You just got to work, and results will come back in loads.'

A kick of booze certainly helps people, to help and advise fellow human beings, most of the time voluntarily.

'Oh! Thanks a lot. Thank you for your guidance Sir,'

'No probs! Enjoy and all the best,' he turned back, and headed straight for the nearest stall of chicken masala curry.

Divaker followed him to the stall; he forgot to ask something very vital. The senior officer turned, and gave a smile. Divaker asked, 'Excuse me Sir, I forgot to ask that where exactly is Meerut located?'

The company gave them very little time to dislocate and join their new headquarters, around a week or ten days. The next day Divaker started his journey back to Papa's place. It took him two days to reach. He told everything that happened during his training, to Papa and Misty. Divaker purchased a big bag to carry clothes and woolens to Meerut, where he was about to start the next very important phase of his life. He stayed there only for three-four days and got no time to visit Maa. He told her everything on phone, and she was happy about this turn in Divaker's life.

On that cold winter afternoon, Divaker started his journey. He sat on a riksha with the big bag and turned back to see Misty, Papa and Moti.

Papa smiled and waved his hand.

Misty kept on wiping her tears.

Moti was scratching near a bush, indifferent. The weak and old riksha-wallah pulled him slowly and slowly away from them.

He met Arif there in Meerut. They were at the same position but Arif was senior to Divaker and also his mentor. After Divaker stayed in a hotel for few days, Arif arranged a room for him on rent.

Thousand-rupee rent per month.

Toilet and bathroom to be shared with the landlord.

A small kitchen that can also be used as a storeroom.

A cot already lying in the room.

Divaker moved into his new world with that big bag, and unpacked things. A Punjabi family in neighborhood ran a hotel in their house, exclusively for bachelors not interested in cooking. A small friend circle developed, all unmarried young men working here and there. Divaker had no short or long-term goals about his life, neither anyone in his friend circle had. He started his day with a heavy breakfast at Punjabi Uncle's house. Throughout the day; he met doctors, distributors etc, and in the evening sat down with friends. Often they boozed to the hearts content and for dinner went to Delhi Darbar – a cheap non-vegetarian hotel. Again the next morning, the next day……….

Life went on like this for a little more than a year. Arif and Divaker could never enter each other's personal zone. They were close, but something amongst them kept them apart. Arif was getting married that year and he invited Divaker to attend his wedding in Allahabad.

Life was somewhat comfortable by that time. Divaker bought a second hand Bajaj scooter for six thousand rupees. He also bought a new cell phone. On weekends, he often visited Gaurav – Delhi was only two hours drive from Meerut. One Sunday morning Gaurav suddenly appeared; he drove all the way from Delhi in his second hand Maruti Car that he had bought from Arman. Gaurav stayed there for whole day and went back in the evening. They had a nice time together, old memories and new happenings. It was like catching up with something that they mistakenly dropped by; a long distance back, in the passage of time.

The old scooter and cell phone were the only things Divaker could buy in that 'little more than a year' time. He ate well, dressed well, and spent his time in the evening well with friends. He was happy and satisfied with everything God had given him. Divaker's boss used to visit Meerut once or twice every month. He kept Divaker charged up, and on the right track. The company gave him hopes for a future and a career to look forward. He saw people growing, and believed that he would also grow. The company rewarded good performance and gave respect to people who did their job well. Divaker got his due from destiny, as for that time, the account was settled.

Arif's wedding day drew close and finally one foggy evening they started for Allahabad – Arif, Divaker and Mridul Bhai. Mridul Bhai was one of their distributors, who got close to them, with his unique ways of sharing his lunch, inviting them on festivals and helping them on closing day by giving orders – not needed – just to meet their targets.

'I have something in the flask.' Mridul Bhai said.

Divaker looked at his flask and understood what he meant.

'I will get some cold drink or soda bottles.' Divaker said.

They started to booze even before the train arrived and carried on in the train too. They had 'paratha' and 'sabzi' for dinner and were soon asleep. Mridul Bhai started to snore with his mouth half open, Arif squeezed his small body in the middle berth, and Divaker spread on the upper berth, his arm hanging out.

Next morning they were in Allahabad, and from that day onwards, events kept on happening as if they were pre-planned.

Going out to find whereabouts of the Mishra family.

Calling up Mishra Uncle's number.

Going to meet them.

Meeting Devyani.

Coming back to Meerut.

Divaker did not fall in love with her that day, but was pleased to see her. She was a frail looking young girl, with curly hair, fluffy cheeks and inquisitive eyes. Something about her was very innocent and childish.

After returning to Meerut he often called them up, most of the time she picked up the phone. They used to chat, but on irrelevant things. She came to Meerut once with Mishra Uncle to appear for a medical entrance exam. They had a wonderful time. By that time, Divaker upgraded to a new bike from his old scooter, it was a 12 bhp motorcycle, and it was just a dream come true for him.

They moved about here and there in the city.

Went to a local fair and exhibition.

Had dinner together in a good restaurant.

Mishra Uncle spent all the time meeting old friends and relatives in the city. Once upon a time, he had spent few unmarried years of his life in Meerut. Next day he went Delhi on some official work.

Divaker got some time in privacy to spend with the young girl, who had just stepped into his life. They were together whole day in the hotel room. Divaker told her everything about himself and his life.

Everything that happened after they left Allahabad.

Things that happened when Papa was posted in Assam.

All the scandalous matter; that compelled Papa to take a long transfer – from Allahabad to Assam.

His high school studies in Patna.

His Graduation in Delhi.

His first job, second job etc etc......

It was like narrating story of a TV serial that somebody had missed on the weekend. Divaker was happy to meet her. They also talked about those days in Allahabad, when she used to come to Divaker's place to play with Misty. That was all a long time back. He had finally found her out after six-seven years.

'Why are you telling these things to me?' she asked casually, as if this thought suddenly came to her mind after listening to everything.

'Nothing, nothing specifically, I had been lonely all my life. Never found a person who would listen and understand. Things just kept on piling in my heart. You had been listening to me so genuinely that I felt like sharing everything with you. Everything just flowed on and on'

She smiled.

They had lunch together and then she slept. After watching TV for some time, she curled on the other corner of the bed and slept. Divaker switched off the TV, and was soon asleep too.

Uncle returned from Delhi in the afternoon. They were to leave for Lucknow the same evening. Divaker presented a pink teddy bear to Devyani. She held her close to her heart all the way from hotel to railway station and in the train also. The train moved slowly and slowly from the platform, and as far as he saw her through the window, she held the teddy bear on her lap lovingly.

8

The Proposal

It was still dark outside.........Days become strangely short during winters, but the nights are long. All this time Divaker had been standing on the terrace staring at the darkness, made darker with the overcast sky. It had stopped raining; bone-freezing winds started whistling, with occasional murmur of clouds and mild translucent flashes of lightning, as if some war is going on somewhere up in the heaven, distant and remote.

'Have you gone crazy or what? It's so cold outside and you are letting all of it raid the room,' Devyani was getting out of the bed.

Divaker closed the door and returned indoor to the warmth and security of the room. The whole room was filled with a sweet scent, personal and moving.

'You were sleeping, I thought better not to wake you up. You too need proper rest, with all the fatigue and job stress, plus the housekeeping stuff,' Divaker said.

'When did you wake up?' she asked.

'Ten-fifteen minutes back,' Divaker said, and eased himself again on the bed.

'Wait I will get some tea,' she said, and moved out of the room wrapping a shawl and walking lazily. Before she closed the door, a gust of cold wind entered the room. Its warm inside and the yellowish glow of bedside lamp made the room comfortable.

Divaker is now in a position to think about life and its event as they happened, the long journey of life from different places with different people. This journey will end, some day, and everything will remain here; and here only, people, places, love, trust, bitterness, everything. All this time he had been trying to hold things in his hand, and not let anything go out of it. One day he has to go, and everything will remain here. Hopes, desires, aspirations, expectations, everything, everything will remain here. Only he'll have to go.

He thought:

Why then I have not lived life fully.

Why then I had always been miser in giving other happiness.

Why did I always think twice before getting happy?

Why didn't I slip in a five-rupee note to the beggar on the railway platform today?

How many times had I been the reason of someones tears?

Or.........

Why do I make Devyani weep, every other day on trivial and insignificant things?

Divaker felt a negative complex building inside him, a fake bubble of 'greatness' swelling in his belly, and traveling up to the throat and then, blop!

He looked at his image in the dressing table mirror in front of him and saw the face of a weak and insecure man. A man bloated with ego, and false sense of greatness. He always expected things to happen the way he wanted. He called it perfectionism, but deep down in his belly – from where the bubble originates- he knew that its nothing, but selfishness and an unnecessary urge to control people, events and emotions and Devyani was the most suffered victim of his fancies. The man in the mirror looked back at him with hate and disgust. He could not keep staring; he turned his eyes away.

Devyani was back in the room with a tea tray in her hand.

'Good one,' he sipped and felt the soothing aroma.

She said nothing, and kept looking at her cup.

'What is Aunty doing?' Divaker asked.

'Getting the dinner ready.'

Her phone started ringing and she got busy with the call. Divaker finished the tea and started playing with his phone.

'Who was that?' he asked, when she hung up.

'None, just my colleague, called up to know whether tomorrow I am taking an off or not.'

'You said you will be going.'

'Yes, actually tomorrow is a restricted holiday. Lot of them taking an off, but somebody has to be there to get things going. I think I would better use it some other time, what do you say?'

'You already said you'll be going. What's the reason of asking me now?'

'But that can be changed; I will again have to call her up. That's all.'

'No don't change your programme,' Divaker said with a look of frustration and anger, very familiar to her.

'Okay, don't be upset now, please. I thought better to keep the holiday in reserve for some other time.'

'What other time?? Do I come here to meet you every other day,' Divaker was irritated.

'Sorry, sorry. I won't go. Ok? When I say something I don't think much about it, you know na?'

Divaker said nothing and kept on playing with the cell phone. She snatched the phone away and looked directly in his eyes.

'Please........don't get irritated. You are here for a day. Please don't ruin your mood Divaker. Please....,' she said pressing her hand on his, and looking right in his eyes.

'Okay, no problem, its okay, just fine,' he whispered without even looking at her. He knew that this part only came out mechanically, like an answering machine.

Press one to record your message.

After getting an assurance that he is all right, she went downstairs to get the dinner ready and help Aunty. Uncle was back from office quite some time back, but did not come upstairs to meet. This was expected from him, as Divaker always saw him this way. Not only with Divaker, but with everyone. He would sit and watch TV, but never walk into the living room to meet guests or visitors, until and unless the visitors would specifically mention his need.

Aunty had a dual role – housekeeper and house owner. Apart from basic needs, uncle would never talk to the girls, neither listen to them. Aunty was also a messenger for to and fro traffic of messages between Uncle and the girls. All the girls are now married, and settled down with their own household in nearby towns. They pay Uncle and Aunty an yearly visit, and call up as and when required, especially on festivals. Devyani was the only girl among them doing a job, and pursuing something apart form looking after her parents. Uncle would retire later this year; Aunty is already a hypertensive and diabetic. Eventually, this not so old couple may need someone to take care.

Divaker wrapped a shawl and went downstairs into the bedroom, attached to the living room. As usual, the TV was turned on; and Uncle sat on his chair, chewing Paan.

'Namaste Uncle,' Divaker said, making himself appear before him.

Uncle walked with all his bulk to the kitchen sink and emptied the contents of his mouth.

'Namaste, what time did you reach here?' he asked, coming back to the room and planting him on the chair again.

'In the afternoon. Was upstairs sleeping all the time.'

'Ok, how is the cold in Delhi this year?'

'It's more here. Maybe the rains, that's why.'

'Ummm,' Uncle said nothing else, and turned the room heater more towards himself.

They all had dinner together – dal, mutton, salad, chapatti, rice – and talked about a TV serial, which Divaker had only heard about. He was a good listener, and Uncle did not even listen to the discussion. He fully concentrated on the dinner. Nobody even bothered to ask him anything or his participation. Uncle is a money making machine that needs food two times a day, most of the monthly income coming down under the table – a socially accepted and appreciated mode of income.

Aunty only knew how to write her name in Hindi, when she was married to Uncle. A foundation school course in Urdu is as good as good as nothing at all. Except for some railway station boards in north India, Divaker doesn't remember where he saw Urdu coming to practical use. The remnants of Urdu can now only be found in some good quality poetry and exclusive Hindustani ghazals, nazms etc. People don't understand, so the poets and writers have taken to a short-cut method – hindi &

urdu remix. Aunty was a mother less child in her adolescent years, starved and deprived of things a girl of her age and background would die for – shiny clothes, cheap bright imitation jewelry etc. She was in late teens when she was married to Uncle, and thereafter she used all her wits and skills to control the man in her life. She bagged a roaring success throughout her life in this mission.

She barely did the household jobs.

Seldom visited the kitchen.

She had piled up enough clothes to last for three lifetimes, and she bought jewelry worth the value of a car.

Obviously, the girls learnt what they saw, except for their own prudence and judgment, the basic framework of their mind was pre-programmed.

Devyani always tried to be different, at least after Divaker met her, she always made efforts to be different from the league of ladies and girls she had seen and lived with, throughout her life – Mummy, Aunties, Cousins etc – but then, genes do have an impact.

After dinner, Divaker and Devyani went upstairs in the other bedroom, without even saying goodnight to Uncle and Aunty. Earlier, Divaker found these things strange, because in his family, Papa and Maa always said good night before going to their room. Even today, he does not acknowledge people missing out on small details in life but then; over years, he had learnt to accept things, peoples, behavior and indifferences.

Divakers family with Papa and Maa was not an organized or ideal family, but they were people who always appreciated smaller things in life. They lived their common life with attention to every possible detail.

'What is your lunch and dinner menu in hostel?'

'How many non-veg meals you people get in a week?'

'What was the character you played in the school drama?'

'Taste of spinach cooked in mustard oil versus refined oil........'

'Color of Bougainvillea flowers in the pot kept on the terrace........'

'How many days did the gas cylinder run this time?'

'Our dog is feeling depressed today, did not have lunch......'

'Taste of carrots grown on the kitchen garden.........'

'etc...etc...etc...'

Lots of similar relevant or irrelevant stuff everyday, throughout the year. They used to talk, laugh, quarrel, then stop talking, and then again talk. Life went on like this for quite some time; until the time Divaker was in his mid teens, somewhere around matriculation, and then the pieces started falling apart. Bit by bit to begin with, slowly picking up speed. They were in Allahabad that time.

Devyani's family was their next-door neighbor.

She used to play with Divaker's sister.

Divaker was a bigger kid.

He never knew that this girl would one day be his wife.

Devyani and Divaker were now inside the same quilt that kept them warm during the day.

'Did you like the dinner tonight?' Devyani asked.

'Yes, very much. I am so fed up with Ammaji's cooking, that any change is a welcome change for me.'

'Does she cook so worse?'

'No, not bad actually. In fact, I am bored of the same type of cooking everyday. Anyway, it's far better than a hotel,' Divaker said.

They were both silent for some time. Both knew that none of them could actually improve the situation.

'Madam, my dessert is awaited,' Divaker said, and pulled Devyani's bra strap. Devyani understood and smiled. She started playing her fingers in Divakers groin.

The presence of a female body near him – warm and fragrant – was a real treat to his senses. He started fondling her through the comfortable cotton nightwear. Soon they were out of the quilt, perspiring, whispering and laughing. They were back in the quilt once it was all over. She kept her head on his shoulders, one leg on him, and was soon in sleepy whispers. A full course of intimacy and lovemaking had drained their energies. Sex without love is half the fun. One needs to love a person deeply to enjoy the full pleasure of intimate togetherness, otherwise it's nothing more than an orgasm, or a masturbation inside a female body. The partner should understand needs, be genuine, and express honestly his or her feeling. Some things develop with time, and can never be found in 'fly by night' relationships, that are so common these days. The satisfaction of making love to the woman one really loves is far far better than picking up an expensive whore in short skirt and small tight top, from PVR Saket or CP.

Divaker felt sleepy, but flashes from all parts of his life started like a powerpoint slide show from God knows where. After Devyani went back to Lucknow from Meerut, with a teddy bear in her lap, they had come up a long way. They used to talk more frequently over phone, sometimes for the whole night. Long distance calling was a bit expensive those days, and the same year Divaker paid mobile bills for around lac rupees – more than half of his annual income. He was madly in love with her. She was a 'naughty brat' kind of a girl, spontaneous and talkative.

She asked stupid questions and laughed.

She listened attentively to all his lectures.

Often she wept.

Then she would complain sometimes.

She was everything Divaker had, and possessed. He did not buy a single piece of furniture, not even a TV. All his disposable income made the cellular company rich. He never repented, not even today.

'At least I have a person who loves me, and I love her.' He would say this to himself. The feeling of real love is simply great. He did not propose her for six months, but then, by that time they had known enough of each other to understand that they were in love.

On career front, he was doing better than average. After one year in Meerut, Arif resigned and went back to Allahabad. Arif now runs a school with his mother. Divaker got a new colleague – a fresh graduate in Business Management. Divaker was now his mentor, and helped him settle down, taught him in and out of the trade, systems and processes in the company. The new guy soon aligned himself with everything. Divaker got due recognition, for shaping up the territory, the new joinee and for performance which was all time high for the area. Good things were happening, he won an 'Award Nite' invitation from the company for all the goodies he was doing – two days in Taj Exotica, Goa. The 'Award Nite' was basically a business meeting in disguise, like a board meeting cum fancy dress competition. He was gradually being accustomed to good things in life. Occasional five star hotel stays, expensive lunch and dinner, air journeys etc. These things made him happy, his long cherished desires turned into reality. This was not a regular lifestyle, but he longed for the flavor of these things for quite sometime. Everything came with a business tag, it's never a full time enjoyment affair, but then he was ready to pay the price as long as he was getting.

He went to Lucknow twice in between for some meetings, and managed to meet Devyani in the evening at her home with all the family around. Six months passed away and their distant relationship grew stronger.

They agreed to meet once, away from the family in a place and time, which would belong exclusively to them. Divaker checked in a good hotel, and picked her up in a cab on her way to college. This time he had something in his mind. He wanted to define the relationship in a formal way. He wanted to take their relationship to the next level of intimacy and understanding. Things not spoken should be said, and heard. Divaker wanted to give their acquaintance the long overdue position and name, which it deserved.

'I am here for a something specific,' he said, when they were settled in the hotel room. Devyani briefed him about all the excitement and tension she had been through that day before meeting him.

'Say, what?'

He was silent for some time.

'I had been thinking about this for quite sometime now. Feelings are not to be kept in heart, and should be conveyed at right time. It avoids misunderstanding,' Divaker said, and looked at her.

She was listening to him intently, looking away from him and smiling.

'Suppose, I send in a marriage proposal to your parents for your marriage with me, how would you react?'

She kept quite, and smiled. She knew perfectly what Divaker wanted to say and knew the answer as well. But, maybe she was enjoying every bit of this climax which genuinely happens only once in a lifetime.

'That is something which my parents have to decide. I will allow them to take decision on my behalf; whatever they feel is good for me,' she said and looked at Divaker from the corner of those big bold eyes, and tried to read out his reaction to what she had said.

'Okay.....hmmm...... that's fine, I know.........,' Divaker was getting tense and his heart pounded fast. He felt a bit insecure too; maybe he was previously in a fake pink and rosy world. Things are not to be presumed and the worst moment of truth was about to dawn, maybe. However, he continued, 'but suppose they give a go ahead, they have no issue, a green signal. What would be your stand? Will you accept me?'

Silence again. The smiles were no longer amusing and Divaker sensed danger lurking around. He could no longer hold on and continued.

'See Devyani, I am in love with you. I love you and I want to spend the rest of my life with you. I don't believe in teenage friendship kind of stuff. I like you, and I want you to be my wife. That's all.'

'Okay,' she said looking at him.

'I could have proposed before also; but then, this was not a matter to be told over phone. I wanted to meet you and say it upfront. Since the time you came Meerut, and then onwards our chatting on phone, I have known and understood you well enough. I like you Devyani. I want to spend my lifetime with you, not months or years, a full lifetime, which I feel is not enough to love you.'

Divaker did not know from where he gathered all of it, but

then he said everything, and was satisfied. He looked at her eagerly and awaited a response. She was deep in some thoughts and smiled without looking at him. Divaker carried on,

'See, you may say that you need some time to think over it, but I can't give you time. You know me for the last six months personally, leave aside the childhood acquaintance. Six months is enough time to know a person, although we could not meet much, but then two hours of average chatting daily for six months would turn out few hundred hours of talking. Don't you think that is enough? Devyani, please, I need your answer today, before you leave this room. If you still say that you need some time, I will think that it's a 'no' from you and carry on with my life. I would carry on with my life. I will think that a wonderful and beautiful person entered my life for sometime and then left, but in no condition, I can carry on this undefined relationship. I need your answer and commitment that you'll be there for me, for my life. Trust me, I won't ask a single question if you don't accept me. I will drop you at home and take the next train to Meerut. The other option is that we keep on carrying this friendship – which I am sure I won't be able to – for as long as it goes. Someday you get married, settle with someone, I get married and I too start a new life. We both get lost in our own worlds, and forget that we ever knew each other. You say how we should go ahead.

He knew that he was doing same mistakes again but he could not help. Basically, a person and his outlook does not change easily.

Divaker was now silent and wanted to hear something from her. After a pause, she said,

'See, first of all this is not only a friendship, but something more than that between us. I have always known that you are someone more than a friend. Your concern for me, your involvement and your commitment for me are more than that of a friend. I trust and depend on you for all the mental support and encouragement. You are the only person whom I can blindly put my faith, knowing that you'll not break it. You are the most reliable person I have ever known. I am always happy with you, and talking to you. I forget that a world outside also exists. I forget all the problems. When you are around I feel myself inside a cozy bubble of warmth and comfort and I forget everything else. I don't know that how will I ever live without you.'

She said this with sincerity and simplicity. Divaker could easily make out that it came straight from her heart. She was not as good a communicator as he was, but this was incredible. He was moved and touched by what she said. It's a wonderful feeling to know that you mean so much for someone. She always used plain and simple language, often not polished, but he considered it a virtue and liked her style. In fact, he loved everything about her. He would never be able to live a life without her. He needs her, and he loves her passionately.

'Would I always mean so much to you Devyani?' he asked.

'Yes Divaker, I think so.'

'I have not got my answer yet.'

'Can't you give me a couple of days?'

'No, I need an answer before you leave this room,' Divaker was impatient, 'if you talk once more about time and thinking over, I will think that your answer is 'no'.'

She giggled and then said,

'Okay, close your eyes.'

He closed his eyes. She put her small and soft hand on his eyelids and said, 'I too love you Divaker.'

He embraced her and kissed her on the forehead. He did not

expect to do this, but it happened all of a sudden.

'I knew that Devyani, I wanted to hear it from your mouth. I would have died if you had said something else.

'How could I have said something else? I would have lost everything that I have today. I can't even think of a life without you Divaker, never ever.'

They kissed each other dozens of time, had lunch together in the room, and talked to their hearts content. They shared parts and events of their life when they lived at two different far off places for few years in between, ignorant of the fact that destiny will someday bring them together once more.

In the afternoon, he dropped her at a place two minutes away from her home. She walked back to her gate and turned back to see Divaker. Her parents would have never approved of their meeting in isolation. Divaker had to go again to meet Uncle and Aunty in the evening.

'Namaste Aunty,' he said when Aunty opened the door.

'Namaste, come in, come in, have a seat. When have you reached Lucknow?'

'I reached here this morning, had some official meeting. I thought better to pay my regards before boarding the train.'

Devyani was watching him from behind the curtain, smiling naughtily. He had dinner with them and then he left for the railway station for his return journey back to Meerut. Devyani stood at the gate for as long as the cab was visible with moist eyelashes.

9

Pleasant Surprise

It was eight o' clock in the morning when Divaker woke up. The sky was clear, and bright sunlight bathed the wet streets and houses. Last night it rained a lot and the clouds lost their existence. He could not recall when he rolled into sleep. As far as he gathered, he had been recalling past events like a slide show.

Devyani was already out of bed, and before he could put on the bathroom slippers, she was there standing at the door with tea tray.

Oh! What a luxury. Bed tea!

'Good morning! When did you wake up?' Divaker was as cheerful as the weather outside.

'Half an hour back. I thought before you wake up I should make some tea for both of us.'

Divaker was utterly happy and she knew that. Fresh days begin with a satisfying nights. He did not say this but she understood. All she had to do was to have a good look at him. Faces say a lot of things, one only needs to read it and understand.

In their initial days, Divaker always said that you know a relationship is working fine if you understand what your partner is thinking only by having a look at him. Lot of things in relationship goes unspoken, said without saying, and understood without listening. A relationship is complete when the other person fills in the gaps you have, and you fill in their empty spaces. It works amazingly, yet it's really simple.

In their case Divaker was a 'voluntary preacher,' always teaching and preaching the best practices of human relationship. Devyani was a silent student. She would listen attentively and reply in monosyllable. Her contribution was too small to call it a discussion. However, her interest and intent to listen was good, which encouraged him to carry on.

Today, when Divaker finds those traits in her, he feels good. She picked up a lot of those 'lecture stuff.' On numerous occasions he felt that their relationship won't be working, its time to call it off, its all over now, and it would never improve, but somehow every time their relationship limped, crawled and gradually stood tall. More than half of this contribution and support came from the other side of the tea tray now.

'How is the tea?' she asked.

'Wonderful, as always,' Divaker said.

'What's the programme for today?' she asked.

'Whatever you say, all yours.'

On free days, they went to some shopping malls, watched movies in a nearby multiplex, did nothing but hang out and had a burger or pizza. Typical metro city stuff. Things that people in the west want to avoid; we go and embrace it. We are a poor nation, and we are more poor due to our 'flock' mentality. We want to think, work, and live the life of goats and sheeps, but never venture out to live a different life. For us the 'flock' means security, bread and shelter. Some of us thrive amongst the flock, most of us live an average life and some of us fall prey to lions and tigers. Divaker was no different; he is also a part of this flock, a face in the crowd of millions of people, unknown and ordinary.

They finished tea, she went downstairs to get breakfast ready, and Divaker went to the bathroom. The sun shone more brightly and dried up the wetness of this mortal world. He opened the door and went to the adjoining terrace. The wind was cold but not chilling as last night. People in neighborhood appeared on their roofs and terrace to gather whatever little warmth the slanting sunlight could give. He pulled a chair from room and sat down on the small terrace. Divaker is now used to the cold off lately, but there was a time when winters simply squeezed the soul out of him. He hates winters, the days are short, even smaller the evenings. He felt lazy, and getting out of the bed is a huge task in winters. He felt hungrier and missed the good warm home food, and above all, he hated the loneliness of night. He missed the warmth and tenderness of a female body by his side. every bloody cold night of December and January.

It was first of December years back, when he proposed Devyani in that hotel room, thereafter he used to come Lucknow almost once every month. He could not afford to pay for a good hotel every time, and also could not afford people staring and whispering when a girl enters a single occupancy room of a ultra budget hotel. Therefore, they met outside, in restaurants, parks and mostly at her home – with all the family around.

They spent their first Valentines day at a friends place. He let them in, handed over the keys, showed the kitchen, toilet, bedrooms and told Divaker -

What to say when the milkman comes.

What to do when the housemaid comes in.

How to manage if anyone drops by.

This guy was one of his friends in Meerut. He belonged to Lucknow, and his parents were out in the village to attend someone's funeral. He obliged Divaker by allowing him to use this opportunity. That friend left Divaker for the full day and went to meet his old classmates.

They did a lot more than just kissing each other that day. Both of them for the first time in life had a proper Valentine day. Divaker still remembers each and every moment of that day. He gifted her bouquet of thirteen red roses, and a pair of earrings. They did not make love, but did a lot of other new, exciting and heavenly things.

Later the same year, when summer was about to leave, and on most of the days the sky was grey, something wonderful happened in Divaker's life. One gloomy humid day of September, he received a call from his boss.

'I need to talk to you for some time. Are you free now?' his boss asked.

'Yes Sir, sure,' Divaker replied with tension building up in his mind, and intestines experiencing zero gravity.

'I am in between the 'Talent Assessment Committee' meeting, and we were discussing you. We have a vacancy in Lucknow for our specialty division. Would you be interested? This position will utilize your skills in a more appropriate way, and this opportunity is in line with your long-term career plans. Would you like to move?'

'I need some time Sir,' Divaker said, uncertain and unable to swallow this big a piece of news.

'Ok, fine. I need to confirm it by tomorrow, call up by evening and inform,' he hung up the phone.

Divaker did not know why he asked for some more time. He already had made up his mind. Job posting in Lucknow was like a dream come true for him, then why did he ask for time. He already had completed around two years in Genetic Biosciences – the US company he worked for – and his career was at a cross road at that point of time. Genetic Biosciences was a growing company. He was performing well, and he knew people who were promoted in a couple of years, giving consistent performance. Saying 'no' would mean staying in the same job role and location for maybe one more year and then expect a promotion. Saying 'yes' would mean a change in job role and location, but then he would again have to prove himself in the new assignment. This new assignment was about selling one specialized product in the immunization segment. The company was doing an experiment on this new expensive vaccine in upcountry market like Uttar Pradesh. The product was doing well in metro cities, but how will it perform in upcountry market was a question. The company always supports someone's movement to a new location or different division or a different job role by saying that it's good for his or her career. Divaker is thinking about all this now, but that time he did not think that much. Divaker asked guys in his trade about the option he had in hand and got mixed opinions.

'Don't take it, wait, you'll be promoted this year.'

'Here at least you know the market, and you can give results no matter what, for at least a year.'

'It's a different selling altogether, specialty products, better exposure.'

'Any increase in salary or allowances?'

'No, there would be no increase in salary and allowances. It's basically a transfer sort of thing. His job group will be the same,' Divaker told.

He did not think much about the professional pros and cons of the opportunity in hand. He was enjoying the tender feeling of staying in Lucknow – the same city where Devyani lives. He had several other things in mind too –

'I do not have to travel all the way from Meerut to meet her.'

'Maybe, I could meet her everyday.'

'I can drop and pick her up from college on my bike, like the way I see other people doing.'

'My long distance calling expenditure will be cut down.'

'We can meet in the privacy of a room without checking in a good hotel.'

'She would not have to go to cyber café to chat with me – and so her chances of meeting someone online will be reduced.'

'If she goes and comes with me from college, nobody will follow her behind the riksha.'

In short, he could see many reasons to take up this opportunity. This opportunity would answer his concerns of insecurity and give him the much-needed proximity to her. And yes, one more reason –

'I will be moving five hundred kilometers nearer to my family, Papa, Maa and Misty. It means one night less in the journey.'

Divaker called up his boss in the evening and told him that he was ready to take up this new assignment.

'See Divaker, whatever I do is a step towards taking care and developing the career of my people. Trust me, you'll grow in this assignment,' he said after he had briefed him about the reporting structure, joining deadlines etc.

The next call he made to Devyani.

'I have good news for you,' he said, pressing his excitement hard so that it does not come out.

'Good news? What?'

'I have been transferred to Lucknow!'

For few seconds she was silent, and then asked whether Divaker was serious, or playing some game, or just whiling away time. He then told her the same thing. She was happy like an excited child.

'I will tell my friends and everybody at home that you are coming,' she said, overwhelmed with joy.

'Okay fine, go ahead. I will be coming this weekend for joining formalities and also to find out a place for me to stay.'

Thc same weekend Divaker went Lucknow. He stayed in a hotel for a couple of days, during which he went to the local office for joining formalities. Maybe out of utter formality Devyani's parents asked him to stay with them, but that was practically impossible. He browsed through the 'TO-LET' column of newspapers and called up half a dozen house owners. He had few requisites like –

Independent one or two room set.

Partially or fully furnished.

Separate entry – no fuss about timings.

No nose poking type of landlord.

Good locality.

Over years of experience, selling various things and talking to thousands of different types of people, he had acquired a fairly good understanding of something called 'human nature.' He short listed people over phone and decided to see two houses out of all those whom he had called up from the 'TO-LET' columns.

Finally, he selected to stay in the second floor portion of a house on the banks of Gomti River. This was a cool and calm colony, situated by the side of embankment road, which ran parallel to the river. It was a sparsely filled in colony of peaceful houses and less noisy streets. His house owner was an elderly lady on the verge of retirement, working in a government office. She had a son and a daughter – both staying in Delhi. She herself stayed in the ground floor with an elderly servant. The first floor remained closed except for housekeeping job and occasional visit of her children and grand children. A small room with a bathroom and a small kitchen was all on the second floor. A big terrace was spread out on the three sides of the room. Access to the second floor was by a winding wrought iron staircase. The window on east opened up to the terrace, and to the beautiful sight of Gomti River.

For two years, that small room was his home. He would walk on the terrace in the evenings and mornings with a cup of tea and feeling – 'What a beautiful world!'

Divaker even installed a small window AC to make his world more comfortable. Gradually and not so smoothly, he was settling down in his new job position. He had a huge area under coverage, which meant ten-twelve days of traveling every month. Divaker was settling down in life. He bought a gas connection, utensils, pressure cooker and stuff of everyday use. He earned well that time, but again his expenses were mounting. Three thousand rupees rent per month, five hundred rupees electricity bill – thanks to the AC, five hundred rupees to the maid and then, the ever irritating mobile bill. The belief that 'phone bill will go down if I start living in Lucknow proved wrong as his phone expenses did not come down, its only that they started talking more over phone.

He had nothing to carry from Meerut, except two bags full of clothes and a quilt. The mattress and the cot belonged to the landlord, so they remained there. He went back to Meerut once to settle down his account with landlord - electricity bill and pro rata rent. He met the distributors with whom he had worked, friends who were not very close, Punjabi Uncle and Aunty who gave him a discount on his last lunch with them, Mridul Bhai, PCO Uncle and many other relevant or irrelevant people. He was not much attached to Meerut, but God knows why he was feeling bad at the idea of leaving the town. Each and every moment of his last day in Meerut reminded him that the people, places and events are all happening for the last time, like a breath which cannot be gathered again, like a leaf falling from a tree, about to touch the ground, irreversible. A strange kind of romance attached with this place or maybe time. He saw the closed door of a house down the lane in his locality and did not see the schoolgirl who would always smile at him. Maybe he will never see her again, ever. This is human nature, not to appreciate things when they happen and understand its beauty once it is gone or about to go.

Akhil was with Divaker for the whole day and took him from place to place on his scooter. He is the guy whom Divaker inducted, the same guy who joined in place of Arif. Events that happened in those two years flashed in his eyes, as he passed the places where they happened.

Roadside Biryani Wala at Hapur adda.

Juice wala at Nai sarak.

There, over there, he had an accident and was hurt badly.

Hotel where Devyani and Uncle stayed and he spent the whole day talking to her.

The liquor shop that closed at 11 PM.

The dhaba where food was available even after midnight.

The road that took them to Khatauli Canal.

Beer, mangoes and naked bathing with friends in the canal.

'I will never forget Meerut,' he said to Akhil, while going to the railway station.

'Do call up and come to meet,' he said turning at the Railway station scooter stand.

Akhil kept on looking away from him, avoiding eye contact. He was smiling, and kept his feelings under wraps of his smile, and thick glasses of minus two point five. He was smiling, but his face told a different story, a story of sharing success, failures, time, joy, sorrow and disappointment. It was like a short story that reached its end at a small railway station of a small town. The expressions on Akhil's face were a brief summary of Divaker's stay in Meerut. A mixture of numerous feelings and emotions, Divaker learnt a lot from that place, and lived life in real terms. He earned money, paid off his expenses, understood life, enjoyed life, understood people and understood himself. His journey for next level had already begun. He played a great innings in Meerut; his next arena was Lucknow – the city where Devyani lived.

They both walked silently under the yellow light of the single sodium vapor lamp. The train arrived half an hour late. He asked Akhil to leave. The train pulled off from the station after some time and he saw the town moving past, and then away, away, and away from him, till it was a group of bright lights amid a universe of darkness. He saw from the sleeper class window a distant cluster of lights, where probably he shall never be returning back.

Next morning he was in Lucknow, in his new cute little world, with a small AC, kitchen, toilet and large terrace. While climbing up the winding iron staircase he felt like climbing a tree and his small room was a nest, up somewhere in the tree.

Yes a nest, a love nest.

The love nest was witness to all their initial lovemaking days. They explored, initiated, and enjoyed love life in their small and cozy love nest. Days that are to be remembered forever, memorable and exciting, mysterious and satisfying, days full of sweet things and nothings.

Divaker caught himself smiling and eyes fixed at vacuum. No idea how much time must have gone by. He was still sitting in the winter sun.

'Breakfast is ready, you better come downstairs,' Devyani shouted from down below.

'Ok, coming,' he replied, but she did not hear perhaps

10

Introspection

Downstairs a sumptuous breakfast of aloo-paratha, butter and curd awaited him. He ate two huge parathas soaked in butter, with curd. No wonder he was putting on weight and his tummy started to show. He never missed the opportunity to feast his tongue, anytime, anywhere.

'Good ones!' Diavker said when he was halfway through.

'Lot of calories, the more you eat, the more you bloat,' Devyani said, nibbling on a small piece of paratha.

He silently finished the curd in the bowl.

'Yes, very true,' he said indifferently, and walked over to the washbasin, a silent belch pulled itself up from the stomach, making way for the paratha and curd to settle down.

He was overweight, by a 'not so big' margin though, but then his tummy was making way, and he could feel the pressure it exercised on the trouser button and belt. Devyani was kind of average, she had put on weight after marriage but that is all the way in a healthy normal range. She had a slim and slithering figure right from the beginning, and Divaker was a bit overweight always.

'Will you fall for a more smart and handsome guy?' he often asked her.

'Why? What's wrong with you?' she would ask back.

'No, nothing. I was just wondering, maybe a more physically good-looking guy may attract you. Moreover, I am not that attractive physically.'

She would laugh and Divaker would look at her face expecting an answer.

'Had it been that way, then why on earth I have fallen in love with you. Physical attraction is not everything and there are a lot of other things which makes me love you.'

'Like……..?' a bit of praise makes everyone happy.

'Come on Divaker! You know why I love you.'

She never praised him for anything on his face, but she was never tired of talking about him to her friends. His little and small ways of caring and loving, made her happy. She never expressed or thanked him for all these things but Divaker knew that each and every small gesture made her happy from within. She absorbed all of it and smiled a bit without looking at him, always, and he knew that his efforts did not go waste. Small and not so significant gestures like –

Waiting outside her college in the sun, for her exams to get over, with a chilled juice can.

Carrying a spare raincoat for her, during rainy days.

Getting her a lunch packet when she stayed full day in the college for practical classes.

Dropping her and then picking her up to and fro the college almost everyday.

These were small things that she never asked for, but Divaker's satisfaction derivative always made him happy. The look of suppressed joy on her face was all that Divaker needed.

'I don't know what to say, you always do so much for me that

I don't even have words to convey my feelings,' she said sometimes.

'No problem, good people should get used to good things in life. No need to thank me. No thanks between us. Your happiness is my happiness,' Divaker triumphantly replied with an aura of greatness around him.

She would observe his face and expressions for some time, and then say, 'Divaker you are spoiling me. Tomorrow I shall be expecting these things desperately. Will you be able to give all your attention and care throughout the lifetime?'

'Yes, why not? If I am this way only, I don't think I will change with time,' he always replied with confidence and assurance, which he used to exhibit in interviews.

That was then, but now having stuffed his tummy with stuffed parathas, relaxing on the sofa with a cup of coffee and his tummy spread out behind the zip of jacket, he doesn't know how much of that confidence and assurance is left.

There had been numerous occasions when he felt, or rather they felt, that their relationship wouldn't be working. Many episodes of insecurity and quarreling over trivial issues every other day, and it was apparent that things can't go on like this forever. They need to either pull off forever, or stay away for some time. Divaker himself understood that on times he had been utterly irritating. There had been times when he behaved or talked in a disgusting manner. He perceived himself as an understanding and liberal partner, but none of his behaviors ever exhibited the fact. He was good towards the relationship, but he had no idea that why he was so stupid sometimes.

After Divaker's transfer to Lucknow, they grew close to each other. They spent a lot of time together, intimately or just moving around. They were a picture of an ideal couple. Eating out, having fun, moving around on motorcycle, taking care of each other, and sharing a single ice-cream cone together. The more their intimacy and proximity developed, the more Divaker's insecurity increased. The insecurity feeling did not occur to him first time after coming to Lucknow. He felt insecure even when he was in Meerut. Whenever they used to chat online, he was doubtful that she might be chatting with other people as well. He used to hide his concern initially, but as their relationship matured, he started asking her shameless questions, with no respect for her feelings.

Today when Divaker sees the development and evolution of his insecurity phenomenon as a third party, he smiles on himself. The first stage was avoiding things. He used to conceal things that he found 'objectionble.'

'I am going to the mall today with friends after college,' she would inform him happily during their chat or over phone.

'Fine, okay. Wind up your work, go back home early and relax,' he used to say nothing but only ask her to get back home early. Meanwhile, his mind was already processing stuff like –

What possibly she could be wearing today?

Maybe she has someone to meet up there.

Is it the mall she is going or somewhere else?

Maybe a group of guys hanging around would flirt with her and eve tease.

He would be restless; processing all this in his mind but never told her the problem and pretended to be happy. This was stage one.

Stage two was a situation in which he exhibited the concern by sounding low but not exposing the real issue. He would simply sound depressed, but not disclose the real concern. She would then ask him numerous reasons for his depressed mood starting from headache to tyre puncture, but the mystery would remain in his heart as if he was doing a great favor by not saying that since she went out to the community park in neighborhood with her sister, he had something like a toothache. He felt ashamed to confess matters like this, and so silence was the best resort.

These two stages however were very short-lived and soon vanished after his transfer to Lucknow.

Stage three was an intermediate stage, consisting of indirect questioning or better defined as 'camouflaged probing method.' Probing methodology without direct questioning like -

'It took you pretty long to come back from college; traffic jam at Nishatganj railway crossing creates havoc at this hour.'

'Sleeveless kurtas are cool in summers, try out some of them.........or have you already tried out?

This stage is again short lived; as the camouflage starts wearing off with time, revealing the raw intent of the questioner.

Then comes stage four, the most pre dominant, irritating, disgusting and long lasting stage of interaction with spouse. This basically consists of queries thrown directly – crude and uncooked – direct from the saucepan of brain in which they simmer.

Questions thrown away straight on the face –

'Where had you been all day long?'

'Why did you not call up? Some other priorities had cropped up. Isn't it?'

'I had been trying to talk to you, who would answer the call? That bloody phone kept on ringing for God knows how long.'

Divaker had nothing to do with answers like –

I was in practical classes.

I was in the bathroom when you rang up.

We are having extra classes these days to complete the syllabus before exams.

These answers gave no consolation to his irritated and disturbed soul. What he was bothered about was whether his expectations were being fulfilled or not. He was utterly selfish with no respect or space for her. He understood vary late that he was grossly wrong, but by that time it was already late, as these small things in day-to-day life increased the distance between them and also decreased respect, tolerance and understanding in their relationship. He did not give her enough breathing space.

It was his helplessness and frustration, which took its toll by eating into the relationship gradually, like a rodent, crunching and munching, wasting more than it could eat. Divaker did not know what, but his justification for all this was that, he loves her and he is concerned about her more than anyone. It is 'this' concern that made him probe and interfere into her life, to an extent that he almost had a bio-data of all her friends entered in his mind. He did not want her to mix-up with 'bad girls', as they would influence her with their 'bad ways.' Divaker almost forgot that she was a grown up adult, and knew how to differentiate between right and wrong. He treated her like a kid, pampering, teaching and preaching every possible good thing one should do in this world.

He treated her like a child, and played the role of a father, in his opinion. But one day, when they were quarrelling over some stupid issue, she asked, 'What do you think I am? What do you think?'

He was silent, wondering that till date she had no idea what does he thinks about her, and what does she mean to him, till he got the answer from Devyani in a voice full of anger and mistrust –

'You think I am some pet, a bitch, and I should always wag my tail, no matter what, isn't it?'

He was shocked, and felt as if a bottle of country liquor had shattered on the floor with its smelly content splattered around, vaporizing all around him. He heard church bells and sirens sounding in his ears from a very very distant place.

Even today, he doesn't know who was right or who was wrong, but this is how their relationship continued, he doesn't know about others. It was painful and agonizing with moments of happiness only when they were together. These moments were in fact few hours of time that they spent together, but the aftertaste carried on for few days, gradually reducing to a couple of days, then only the day they met and then..............pathetic.

Divaker thought that he was the most caring and loving husband and lover in this world, never did he imagine that their relationship would gradually turn this way, causing frustration, and take away peace of mind. He knew why it all happened. It all happened due to his insatiable urge of control over everything. Control over people, places and incidents. We all hate failures, in whatever form they appear in our life. Failures big or small make life miserable. Day to day life gives us a taste of success and also compels us to lick the bitter potion of failure. It is all up to us, to understand and swallow the bitter part of life as a medication – a potion – that gives us the ability to relish the honey of success. It works identical in relationships also. It's not a part of cardboard puzzle game, where the pieces fit exactly into each other but somewhat like an odd shape pillow – you need to adjust both your neck and the pillow, throughout the night, and keep cursing, but most of the time you forget all about it when you wake up fresh in the morning.

Divaker tried to control his life, his relationship, and be the creator of his own happiness, with all resources put together, his time, money, commitment, desires and probably his future also. He expected their relationship to give back exactly what he had put into it, but things don't work out the way one wants. These things depressed him, frustrated him, caused him headache and set his mind in a dizzy.

Divaker realized that he had been holding the empty coffee mug for pretty long.

The sound and aroma of cooking flowed from kitchen to all parts of every room. He peeped inside the kitchen and kept the coffee mug alongside other used utensils in the sink.

'Need some more?' Aunty smiled and asked, crackling some cumin seeds in a frying pan.

'No thanks Aunty.'

He went and peeped in the room where the TV remained on all times of the day and Uncle watched it, irrespective of programme or preferences. Devyani was not there.

He went to another room, it was dark and she was not there also.

Divaker then went upstairs and pushed the door. He saw Devyani going through piles of papers and talking on phone. She looked at him and continued with the call. He was expecting some non-verbal reaction from her, but she did not seem to notice him. He sat on the bed for some time, and then went to the terrace, where he faintly heard Devyani talking and giggling on the phone. Had it been old days he would have asked –

You did not even ask me to sit down.

So the call is more important than I am, isn't it?

She never made him feel that he was more important than

anyone, was or damn anything else on earth. Be it the least important thing in world, Divaker was the object to be parked until the time she would be free and over with her 'important thing'. They quarreled over such matters a dozen times and she would reply –

So, you mean that I should not talk to my friends.

You mean that I should leave my studies, friends circle and lock myself up in a room.

All you want is to alienate me from rest of the world.

He had no answers to such reasoning. The only way he could defend was again give a lecture on understanding, expectations and priorities. Over time, he realized that his lectures just rolled and fell to the ground like water droplets from goose feather, and then gradually he stopped saying anything at all.

'Things not understood are to be skipped over.'

He made many efforts to make her understand that it's natural for him to expect behaviors that he himself exhibited like –

Being very brief on office calls when she was around.

Not wasting 'precious' time of togetherness talking to anyone else.

Even if he had to take up a call, apologizing for the time 'wasted'.

Making her feel that 'I am around' with body language.

Exhausted, he slowly gave up and accepted things he could not change. His heart although could not accept but he compelled his mind to gulp down the bitterness of compromise.

Things kept on piling like a garbage pit and increased the distance between them.

Leaning on the railing of terrace, his eyes looked at nowhere and his ears still heard faint giggling and talking from inside the room. She hung up after some time.

'What are you doing on the terrace?' she asked with sudden realization and curiosity.

'Nothing.'

11

The Silent Pain

When he had completed around a year and a half in Lucknow, parents on both sides started talking about their marriage. They had spent good enough time in their affair for everybody to know. They had meanwhile seen enough of lovemaking, romance and an unexpected pregnancy.

'You guess!' Divaker asked her hiding the test strip like a pearl in his palm.

'I don't know. No idea, but the anxiety is killing me.'

He opened his palm, and the test strip smiled at them maliciously with two dark strips, lurking out of a tiny plastic mouth, wet with urine sample.

Divaker was as anxious and stressed as she was, but at that point of time his job was to ensure that she remains cool and collected. He knew that he had two options; firstly, a quick-fix marriage and secondly, an abortion. The former was difficult but not impossible, difficult because Maa and Papa stayed at two different places. Only once did they appear together at his place in Lucknow, talked about the marriage with Devyani's parents and then vanished. Papa and Maa had no urgency on their part to get Divaker married. Marriage means liability and expenses, which everyone wants to avoid. Devyani's parents were satisfied to have finalized about the marriage with Divaker's parent. They had no intention to get Devyani married off in near future. They were just free from the marriage of their eldest daughter only three months back, and wanted at least a year to prepare themselves for the next marriage.

Given this scenario, it was really difficult for them to materialize the marriage thing, although not impossible. A decision like urgent marriage required a lot of bold decisions and hard initiatives from both the partners. It would also mean that not everyone in the family would be grinning, and blessing the newly wed couple. They had to think out of the box, beyond normal, and be mentally prepared to face everything that comes their way.

The second option was comparatively easy. Divaker had to find out a lesser-known Gynecologist in some remote part of the city, pay consultation and pretend being a newly married couple. Then discuss the problem of missing periods. She would then ask to do a pregnancy test and the results would surprise them. They will exhibit a fake expression of mixed reaction and admit that they do not plan to a have a baby so early. The doctor will then advise on ways and means of 'getting rid' of their concern. They will then ask for few days to think about it, acting in a way as if it's really hard for them to take such a step.

He told Devyani about both the options they had, and the proceeding events and consequences. They were both silent for some time. Divaker did not know which way to go. His heart was always strong over his mind, and he was simply amused at the idea of the baby, who was maybe just as small as a pea or a walnut – a sapling inside the person whom he loved and made love. Then he also thought about how to fix up a marriage in a little less than a months time. They will have to compromise on many things –

A very small list of invitees.

A simple dinner arrangement.

Not too many clothes or jewelry.

Nothing lavish or grand as people imagine and hope their marriages to be.

In fact, everything a bit below normal, a bit compromised.

'But, I always imagined that I will invite all my friends and relatives in my marriage, and that it will be a big celebration type of event, and I will dress up like a princess................,' Devyani said disheartened.

'Yes, everyone hopes and dreams of a fairy land marriage, but then real life is quite different Devyani. Things do not always happen the way you want or hope,' he assured her pressing her close to his shoulders.

She was silent for some time.

'What will happen to my exams? They are only two months ahead; I will have to lose this year. With marriage on the cards, and exams a month after, I don't know how to manage.'

The next day they were waiting to consult a Gynecologist, in a locality where chances of someone acquainted with them coming across all of a sudden was nil. This lady doctor was well qualified, but not so well known. Her compounder was an old lady who kept on staring at them, reading their thoughts or relationship. She perhaps understood why Divaker and Devyani were there, and Divaker was over acting the role of husband.

Thereafter, everything happened just as he had imagined.

'Please don't delay this matter, as it would further complicate things, and meet me with the ultrasound report tomorrow, then only I can advise on how to proceed,' the middle age gynecologist said in a cold tone.

They saw another couple entering the doctor's chamber when they were leaving.

Next morning they were at an USG lab, for a full bladder USG of lower abdomen. The clerk at the cash counter looked at Devyani first, her lower abdomen and then at Divaker.

Divaker was going through times he had never imagined. This kind of humiliation happens when a person is not true to himself. He felt disgusted and humiliated.

Devyani would lie like a corpse when Divaker used condom while lovemaking and upon insisting to have oral contraceptive she said, 'I will gain weight, I don't want to be on OC's.'

The only preventive measure between them was doing sex on safe days or ejaculating outside. In this scenario, it had to happen one day, and this was the day.

Divaker did not understand much of the USG report and took it to the doctor.

'It had been forty-seven days. Doing hormonal manipulation may be risky,' she said.

'You suggest madam. I wanted to simply avoid any kind of surgical intervention,' Divaker said.

Next ten minutes she tried to sell him the benefits of surgical procedure over hormonal, and he listened, understanding things only relevant to him. She also said that hormonal manipulation might lead to unpredictable result and complications. It's better to leave things over to someone who really understands the stuff, so Divaker agreed to what she had been trying to convey. The doctor felt relieved.

'You people come in the morning and bring her empty stomach.

You can go back by afternoon. The procedure does not take more than forty-five minutes, plus she may need some time to cover up the anesthesia effects,' the doctor informed them.

'How much for the whole thing?' Divaker asked.

'People get it done for as low as five hundred rupees to as high as five thousand rupees. I charge two thousand five hundred,' she smiled and looked at both of them one by one.

Divaker had completely understood the benefits of surgical intervention, he agreed.

'When can you plan it out? Means, there is no use delaying it. The faster the better,' she again confirmed.

'Tomorrow?' Divaker asked Devyani, and she nodded her head gently.

Next morning Divaker withdrew five thousand rupees from his bank ATM – that was all the money he had in his account, and went to the doctor. The doctor worked from her home. Her drawing room was the patient waiting area, a bedroom was converted into consultation room and Divaker later realized that another bedroom was used as an operation theater. He tightly held Devyani's hand until she entered the so-called OT bravely, with the old lady – who switched roles between receptionist, compounder and a nurse also.

Divaker sat in the consultation room with only a door in between, that separated the 'OT' and the consultation room. For next forty-five minutes, he heard muffled voices of the doctor talking to the old lady, something electrical switching on and off, and sound of steel equipment clattering and doing its job.

After an hour, Devyani was brought out of the 'OT' on a stretcher, and moved to another adjoining room – it had two beds – this was the postoperative ward. He saw Devyani's eyes closed and she was wearing a bottle green OT gown. Her mouth was half-open and saliva rolled out of it. Divaker wiped off the saliva with corner of his shirt. The old lady accompanied her. She put a blanket on her.

'She may experience chills, effect of anesthesia,' the lady informed and walked out of the room.

Divaker tucked the blanket properly around her, sat on the other vacant bed, and watched her half-open eyes.

'She will be okay soon, in half an hour. If she feels like eating something, give her tea and biscuit. Nothing heavy, as she may throw out,' the doctor said, and asked Divaker to come to consultation room.

She wrote a prescription of antibiotic and asked him to get a USG done after fifteen days again. Divaker paid her cash and again sat on the bedside for half an hour, wiping the saliva coming out of her mouth.

Not even in his worst dream did he visualize this day. He felt pity on Devyani, and on himself. He did not know what kind of impact this incident was going to bring to their relationship. A constant disturbance and turmoil was going inside him, but this was time for him to be patient and calm. He wanted to support her in every possible way. He did not want to see her disturbed or depressed. He did not want her to carry a sense of guilt. He wanted her to take this incident very lightly, and forget it with time. An emotional trauma at such a tender point of time and age could bring devastating results for a girl who still had no idea of the world, and people who inhabit it. He watched her and kept on thinking.

After half an hour, she faintly murmured his name, and vomited out an ounce of saliva and mucous – the doctor had asked her to come empty stomach for the procedure. Divaker drew close to her and put his hand on her forehead. She was shivering. He packed the blanket properly around her. After some time she slightly opened her eyes, but did not seem to recognize him. She repeatedly whispered his name and held his hand tightly. He tried talking to her. Meanwhile, the old lady peeped inside the room to take stock of situation.

Another half an hour went, and Devyani started talking. The lady came again.

'You can take her home now. Let me change her clothes. Tea and biscuit can be given at home also,' she said with urgency, as if she wanted them to leave as early as possibly.

Divaker helped that lady take off the bottle green gown. Devyani was conscious and understood what was happening. A thick cotton pad was stuffed in between her thighs.

'Remove it once she is comfortable at home,' the lady said.

The doctor also entered, and observed him helping Devyani put on clothes like a mannequin.

'Its all right now, she is fine. Had it happened earlier also, sometime in the past?' the doctor asked.

'Why? No doctor, never,' Divaker said.

'No, actually I noticed some scar sort of mark inside, maybe some infection or something. Anyway, take her back home and let her relax for the whole day. Something light to eat during the day and a light dinner at night,' she said and went back.

Devyani limped slowly out of that tiny nursing home. He helped her come out, and asked an autoriksha to stop. All the way, she was half-asleep and rolled her head repeatedly on his shoulder. The autoriksha driver observed them all the way in the rear view mirror and Divaker kept looking away, avoiding eye contact. They were back to the room – the love nest.

Fortunately, no inquisitive neighbor saw them at that hour of afternoon. Devyani's condition would have triggered anyone's thought process. She again slept for an hour. She felt better when she woke up. Divaker made her a cup of tea. She sipped half of it and had a piece of wheat flour biscuit. It was three o' clock in the afternoon, time for her to get back from college.

'Can you hold yourself on the bike?' Divaker asked.

'Yes, sure. No problem. It's alright now, just a bit of pain down under.'

She sat with him on the motorcycle. Divaker asked her to hold him strongly and drove slowly-slowly, avoiding bumps and bad roads. She got down ten steps away from her home.

That night on phone, Devyani asked him all that happened after she was out of the OT, unconscious, and Divaker asked her all that happened when she went inside and before anesthesia was given.

'Better forget everything that happened today as a nightmare. Let's never talk about it again, ever in our life. Nothing ever happened like this to our life, nothing. Okay?' Divaker said.

'Okay.'

For few days, a silent pain prevailed in their relationship. He knew that she felt bad about the whole thing. He knew that she could never forgive herself for what happened and he also knew that she did not have the courage to take up the other path – difficult and bold one. A week went by.

'I wish, I could have seen him, or her, I even don't know what as it, whether a boy or a ....' she could not complete.

'I told you that let's forget all about it. Nothing ever happened. Incidents like this happen with many people. Don't carry the backlog of past and spoil your present. Nothing ever happened. No use beating the bush now. We should have thought about this before visiting the doctor, Devyani. Isn't it my heart? It was just a bad dream for both of us. Let's promise not to let any such thing ever happen in our life again. Don't feel bad. After all, 'Almighty' does everything. What really matters is how strong our relationship is, and how do we support each other in times of crisis. Are you getting me, sweetheart?' Divaker tried his best to comfort her.

She listened to each word intently, and then said, 'Yes, true, very true.'

Since that day, they never raised that topic between them. It was only once that he asked her to get another USG done; as a normal follow up to the procedure, but she declined saying that everything is fine now. She had a normal spotting period after another few days and life soon recovered as if nothing really ever happened. Time is a great medicine. It not only heals wounds visible superficially, but also those wounds, which are far too deep rooted down to the memory lane of mind or to an injured corner of traumatized heart.

Those days Divaker had some problems with his job too. In few months, he had taken too many off days to attend personal priorities. He was not able to cope with changing environment and mounting pressure. The zeal and passion in work, which everyone once appreciated, had gradually vanished. He was not able to bring results as he used to previously. Expectation from bosses and company kept on increasing. Initially, he thought that it was just a seasonal variation, and that things will improve automatically, but Divaker soon found himself in a noose that tightened more, as he tried to get free.

Divaker was losing concentration and focus from basic things in life, like his job, which was the powerhouse of all his needs and finances. He did not have a strong family background; he did not have financially strong parents on whom he could 'fall back' at bad times. He could not make a healthy saving account in bank, nor did he have an investment base to depend or plan his future. Divakers parents went back to their own places, after having stayed with him for around a month. They had fixed up his marriage with Devyani with no specific date or year, and then they went back. They went back to their places and said that they had an 'earning son,' who could not even buy them a pair of shoes, or a saree.

He was twenty-four years old.

Expectations are a complex set of human behavior. No relationship could ever exist without it. Fulfilling expectations makes one happy. Getting expectations fulfilled makes one happy.

The amount of expectation keeps on mounting until it reaches a threshold, and then all the parties in this expectation game lose interest. The same thing was going to happen in his life also. He although did not have an idea about it.

12

A Good Night

The sun had started turning pale and its rays formed slanting shadows that will keep on getting long and long and long, until the sun gets lost somewhere in the dust of western horizon, like a fifty paisa coin, suddenly slipped out of the wallet at a cigarette shop, and vanished in the dust.

Nothing,

Yes, nothing.

Divaker had been doing nothing since morning. He had a sinfully rich breakfast of aloo paratha, curd and butter. He spent some time on the terrace and then he dozed off.

Sometimes, doing nothing is the best thing to do, especially considering his nine to nine routine in Delhi. A fucked up busy schedule of running here and there, meeting people and deadlines, responding and reading mails, taking up two dozen phone calls a day, preparing and giving presentations, seeing same faces at the cafeteria, hearing same stuff everyday and breathing the stale office air in the irritating white light of fluorescent lamp.

Its exhaustive and stressful enough make a person impotent.

A day out of his ordinary and hectic life is like a breath of fresh air. He was feeling guilty at letting his mind and body relax to this proposition. But one needs to unwind and see the other side of life which is far from the daily grind of activities.

Devyani came out of the bathroom, having taken bath, brushing and combing her hair

'Are we going somewhere or just letting the day pass, sitting and relaxing all the time?' she asked, when she saw him fixed to the terrace.

Divaker moved from his place, took a towel and went to the bathroom. The touch of warm water on his naked skin comforted the soul. He took a lazy bath, and enjoyed every bit of running warm water.

There in Delhi, he doesn't have a geyser fitted in the bathroom. As a single man, how much of household could he accommodate and accumulate? Devyani stayed with him for a little less than a year after marriage, and then came back to Lucknow for her job. After that, when he started living separately, he did not feel like accumulating and purchasing household things. He had more than what he required, and had no long term or short term plan of how he could get things in place.

Divaker and Devyani decided to have lunch outside. A new shopping mall had come up with a McDonalds counter on ground floor. He took car keys from Uncle and started the engine of an outdated 800cc car that cluttered and rattled for a while before coming to life.

The place was full of people; most of them had come to catch a movie or just hang around. The shops inside were leading a life on ventilators, waiting for customers, whereas the central area and parking was full like a platform of New Delhi Railway station. He slowly turned the wheel and parked at a vacant space, took the parking token and walked out into the open area in front of the mall. Devyani held his hand, fingers criss-crossed into each others hand.

The picture of a perfect couple.

'Let's get some corn?' Divaker said as the aroma of steamed corn entered his nostrils with a whiff of air, just as he entered the mall.

'Why do you always feel like eating?'

'Come, we will take one and share,' he said, pulling her to the corn stall.

They did a little bit of shopping; chewing those buttery-peppery steamed American corn – that's what they call them – Divaker did not know the farmer who cultivates them, and the village from where those corns came.

He bought a pair of socks, shaving cream, and she bought some grocery. They knew their own requirements so there was no need of discussion regarding what to buy and where to buy. The commodities had to be used differently, and at two different places. Therefore, no need to take unnecessary suggestion or interfere into what the other person was buying. Say, Divaker preferred an Indian brand of corn flakes, but she bought Kellogs, because Divaker was not the person to have breakfast every morning with her.

Small little things happened every other day during the initial years of their relationship. It happened once that they met at Hazratganj Market. She was wearing a tight trouser and a top that was short enough to reveal her waistline. Moreover, it also revealed parts of her undergarment on various occasion. Divaker did not know whether that was intentional or not but he was furious.

'What happened? Suddenly what happened?' she asked.

'Nothing.'

'You came here happily but suddenly started looking upset.'

'Yes, maybe, but I am alright.'

'Everything was fine, but the moment you saw me, your face swelled up like a toad. Is it something that happened back in the office? Ummm.......or that you were doing something important and you had to spare out time to meet me. Isn't it?'

'No, not exactly,' he mumbled back.

Divaker had been thinking all the time that how to make this stupid girl understand the real issue. He wondered whether she really had no idea of what had turned him off. He had spoilt his mood, as well as her mood also, and ruined a day, which otherwise could have been a fun filled one. Divaker's face looked like a boiler, puffing out invisible steam from ears. The more he saw her irritating trouser and occasional glimpse of undergarment girder, the more steam came out of his ears.

'Please tell me what happened?' she asked again, holding his hand tightly.

'Nothing! Bullshit!'

'I know, you got irritated because I called you up and asked you to meet. Actually, I wanted you to see me in the new dress that I bought last year. I never wore it. I thought you might like to see me wearing it. That's why I called you up. Anyway, sorry, but please don't be upset. You can catch up with your work tomorrow. Okay?' she said and smiled, looking at him.

Divaker said nothing, and watched other people observing them. Few of them zoomed their bloody eyeballs to the opportunity of seeing stuff that is generally not visible in broad daylight.

He dropped Devyani somewhere near her house. The whole

day was ruined and spoilt. He missed work, and she too had a burnt day. They did not talk anything on the way back. Divaker was riding, and imagined the entertainment of drivers driving in the same lane behind him, nobody keen on overtaking.

She spent a lot of time to get the issue out of Divakers stomach, when he called her up that night. She listened to everything he said, silently and did not interfere.

'It took you so long to share with me such a small thing,' she said, when he was through with his stock.

'Small thing?' he asked.

'Yes, I did not know it was happening at all. Everyone wears trouser or low waist jeans these days.'

'You were showing your bloody panty out to the world and you say it's a small thing. Isn't it? You think I should grin and clap every time it was visible?' he was loosing temper.

'Do you think I am that kind of a girl? If at all something like that was happening, you should have told me about it immediately. I would have done something about it.'

Divaker said nothing. He knew that opening mouth means spilling out venom.

'I did not know something like this was happening. If I had been aware, I would never have put on this trouser. Maybe it's a year old and I have gained a bit weight, that's why. I never wore it since the days I bought. Do you think I would love doing such dirty stuff? What do you think I am? Tell me, what do you think about me? Why did you not say anything when you first saw? I could have come back straight to home. You allowed everyone to see and meanwhile you were building a pressure within yourself, so that when given a chance you can show me how cheap and disgusting creature I am. Isn't it?'

Divaker had nothing to say anymore. His stock was finished. He was now feeling bad about the whole thing. She was at the verge of weeping.

'Please, don't weep Devyani. Please don't weep,' he said.

'Today I realized how much respect you have in your heart for me and what is my image in your eyes,' she started sobbing.

On phone, he could not see but both of them had developed skills to visualize and understand the mood, expressions and face of the other person, just by listening.

'No Devyani. It's not that way. Please stop weeping. Actually, I felt bad about it. I don't want anyone to stare at you lustfully. You know pretty well Devyani that I am not able to express things the way it should be expressed. I understand that it causes problems, but that is a basic part of my personality, which is not easy to change. Further, I was irritated to see that you were least bothered or concerned. That's why. Please.........Devyani, don't weep,' he made an effort to get things in place.

After apologies, lot of convincing and promises, she stopped weeping. For another half an hour they had a goodie-goodie kind of chatting. Problem over for the day. They exchanged good night kisses over phone. She was again happy, as if nothing ever happened and they both slept, in their own houses.

Today, this incident suddenly flashed in his mind, when he saw a girl wearing a dress with both bra straps revealed and visible. Actually, the dress was designed in a way to make them visible. Devyani was wearing a fine starched cotton short kurta, terracotta pendent and leather slippers. She was the woman he had always dreamed about, classy and elegant. She looked attractive.

'Like to have some more corn?' he asked.

'No, got to have something for lunch too.'

They bought a grilled chicken burger, fries and a large coke – with more ice cubes than coke. They also checked out what's running at the multiplex, and decided to watch a movie. He was happy, and she too was happy. There was a whiff of romance between them after a long time. The way of holding hands, touching each other, gives a feedback of attraction and longing. This is a language, which is understood by every couple in the world, and they were no exception.

Divaker asked himself-

Why every day is not as beautiful?

What are things that create difference and distance?

What are the missing elements of our life?

What are the things that make me feel incomplete?

How to fill in the vacuum, which gradually drains off my energy, enthusiasm, passion and life?

There are couples who stay at different places. There are priorities and requisites, which needs to be taken care of. After all life is not a never-ending fairy tale of togetherness and romance. Harsh realities of life that certainly needs to be accepted and digested. Is he the only loner in this damn world to confront issues like this? Or, are there people who face the same question every day of their life.

They say 'be a part of the solution, not the problem,' he doesn't know who said this. Its easy for anyone to teach and preach. Everyone listens to a person who is a management guru, had been a high flying corporate, gives motivational presentations round the world and then writes a book with a catchy title and smiling photograph.

What about those matters where the question itself is a part of solution, and the solution a part of the problem.

Who will take care of Devyani's parents, if she comes along to stay with him? Are parents to be deserted at old age, in pursuit of personal happiness? As far as Divakers parents are concerned, they have lot of problem and mentalities to cope up with first.

What about the well secured job she had in hand, and he, in an insecure private job, where every bad month sets the warning bells ringing.

What would happen to all her sleepless night of studies? If she had to end up being a full time housewife, cooking and housekeeping, why did she do a masters degree?

It was dark when they came out of the theatre. Days in winters are considerably short. The movie was all about neo-patriotism where heroes fight against bureaucracy and the unfortunate political scenario of the country. Patriotism gave us freedom from British rule fifty-nine years ago. Now who is going to free us from corrupt politicians, ineffective law enforcement and stupid bureaucrats? We need a whole generation of patriots.

'Gosh! Its so chilling, the winds,' Devyani said.

'True,' he said, and pulled one of her cold hand in his pocket of the jacket.

They walked close to each other rubbing shoulders; he put his hand on her shoulder and pulled her close. She smiled. They got relief inside the car, at least from the freezing winds.

'Should we take something for Uncle and Aunty,' he asked.

'No, dinner must be ready. No need to buy anything for dinner.'

Divaker drove for fifteen minutes listening to a romantic number on car radio from the same movie they watched, and talked about the 'goods' and 'not so goods' of the movie.

'You are in a wrong profession. You should have been a film critic,' Devyani said.

'Yeah true,' he laughed, 'a salesman and a film critic.'

They reached home, and changed their clothes to comfortable home wear.

'You people should have at least called up to inform that you'll be late,' Aunty complained.

'It was all of a sudden that we planned for the movie,' Devyani said.

'But yes, we could have made a call,' Divaker said, understanding that a call wouldn't have been a big deal when they were carrying two cell phones. It was carelessness on their part and there was no use defending it.

'Yes, we had been wondering why it's taking so long for you to get back. I also thought maybe you'll not have dinner at home,' Aunty raised her reason to worry.

Devyani looked at him, perhaps thinking what he was thinking, and thought that it's better to resolve doubts.

'So, do we have something for dinner here?' Devyani asked doubtfully.

'Yes, sure, that's why I was worried. If you have had dinner outside, my cooking would have gone waste,' Aunty replied.

All of them watched TV. They talked more and watched less, as Uncle kept on swapping channels endlessly. Nobody was actually watching, and the TV only filled in the gaps of conversation.

They had a homemade combination of roti, mutton qorma, biryani and raita. As a normal trend in their home, they had planned to eat at different timings, but Divaker insisted everyone to come together and they all had dinner together.

After dinner, Divaker and Devyani went upstairs, closed the door behind and switched off the lights, except the night lamp. It was warm inside and the dim yellow light of night lamp made the whole environment cozy and soothing. They pulled the quilt all over, up to the neck and felt for each other's warm body. Fingers, toes, nose and ears were still cold.

She clasped him like a child and pressed her face sideways on his chest. Divaker smelled her hair and kissed her black locks. They did not talk or speak anything. They were completely warm and Divaker enjoyed moving his hand on the bare surface of her tender and soft skin, marked by goosebumps here and there. She enjoyed the movement of his hand on her naked body, and shuddered a bit when he touched her more tender areas. After some time, it was not his hands, but tongue and lips doing the same thing. She was hysteric with pleasure.

They started sweating after some time, and the quilt rolled over to the floor. At the peak of lovemaking, the language of love is not words, but various sounds that have their own meaning. When they reached the top of the world and everything material seemed to lose significance and when time and space seemed to merge, forming a single entity, he heard her whisper, eyes closed and her naked body trembling:

'I love you, Divaker.'

Tomorrow he has to leave for Delhi.

13

The Change

Midway between their affair before marriage, he quit the job. He could not do well in the assignment on which he was sent to Lucknow. Pressure for performance was mounting day by day and he was no longer enjoying work. He had to travel ten-twelve days every month, he worked very hard but in spite of that, yielding results had become next to impossible. His boss used to come from Delhi. Seeing that the business contribution from his area was flat, and not growing, he reduced his twice-monthly trips to once monthly, and then once every quarter. With no support or guidance, Divaker was left all alone to cope and handle the situation.

Divaker had worked on that assignment for two years and in those two years, he had developed enough rapport with his customers to drink and dine with them. Acceptance of his vaccine was theoretically good with them, but out of ten-fifteen patients, only one could afford, and before the product was established, the market flooded with generics at one-fifth the price of his product. In a cost sensitive market like U.P, this was doomsday for him and his vaccine. He could have fought back with passion and commitment, but then, the zeal and enthusiasm that he previously had, was lost somewhere. He had heard someone say that employees don't leave companies, they leave their managers. Maybe it's true.

In Meerut, Divakcr had a boss who was young and energetic like him. His involvement in field activities and associates was very high. When Divaker raised a topic in meetings or presentations, he knew exactly what Divaker was talking about and accordingly suggested ways of either getting rid of the problem or improvising upon a certain aspect of the job. Divaker's present boss was a different person. He would make field visits, customers calls, but he never gave any feedback. He would play game on his cell phone before an appointment and seemed lost somewhere. He showed no signs of interest in the territory.

'Please suggest on how to go ahead. This is my plan.........what do you say?' Divaker often asked him.

'You are a senior person now Divaker, you know better how to handle your territory and customers. I am only a tourist. It's up to you to take corrective steps, plan and implement strategies that suit your market and customers,' he would reply, and get back to the phone game again.

His boss gave only one feedback while on railway station, going back to Delhi.

'We expect a lot from you, but somehow the fun is not visible in your market. Water if flowing above our heads now.'

The next day his boss would send a mail from his posh cabin in Delhi, with a couple of good things to begin with, and then a list of unsatisfactory observations that he had found during his visit to Lucknow. Divaker had started feeling the suffocation. He saw no use of working hard, taking risks, walking the extra mile. Had he been in Meerut, by that time he would have been promoted, but then, maybe destiny had fixed up something else for him.

He had few things lined up in his mind as a future career option. One thing was for sure, he was going to quit the job. He could no longer carry on with a job where his efforts are not recognized and his self-respect was at stake.

He had planned to run a car rental company of his own. He discussed it with Devyani, but she did not agree with his decision. From her point of view it was always safe to be on a job, at least the salary cheque comes in every month end, unlike business where nothing is certain. She had seen her Papa in government job throughout her life and had no idea that a private sector job is more insecure than running a business of your own.

The big managers of big companies grin in meetings and say, 'Change is necessary.' Divaker also agreed but this truth is applicable to both sides of the coin. He should definitely change with the job environment, market and geography, but then things should also change for him, like a change in job role, job profile etc. He was fed up being a salesman for all those long years. He wanted some change to happen in life. He wanted to jump out of the rat race tracks. He was fed up of catching the late night train to Varanasi on foggy and chilling winter nights. He was fed up of returning home an hour before dawn, and then taking antacids to press down flatulence. He was fed up of meetings that went on formally until seven in the evening, and then informally until mid night, in guise of cocktails and dinner. He was also fed up of waiting at railway stations, and checking in at all types of hotels.

One day, during autumn, Divaker called up his boss and asked him to receive a fax on the other number. This was Divaker's one-month resignation notice as per company norms.

For the next two days, people from office called up many times.

His boss called up half a dozen times.

The HR head called up.

His ex-boss called up.

All of them asked him to rethink over his decision of quitting the company. They all showed him how a golden future awaits him next year.

Divaker agreed to everything they said, but he had already decided to walk out with dignity, before his respect is thrown inside the ground for everyone to play football.

After an online exit interview, his resignation was accepted, and people immediately forgot him as if he never existed.

For one full week, he did nothing. He enjoyed every piece and moment of newly discovered freedom and life. He had some financial backup, which had cropped up from a money-back life insurance policy that month. He gave all his time and attention to Devyani during that period. He loved her, and pampered her the way he had always imagined, without the tension of missing work, or the reports that had to be mailed back everyday from an internet café.

They were both extremely happy, except some concern from Devyani regarding his future. He was more happy, as he no longer had to return by mid-night trains. Previously Devyani never slept until she was assured of his return to the room safely, and often Divaker used to be out of cellular coverage area. It used to be a restless wait for both of them. He had sorted out these problems.

Divaker even escaped on a two days quick vacation on the hills. It was impossible for Devyani to come along.

He fulfilled his dream of having beer on a hammock with a Sidney Sheldon novel in hand. Nainital is a fabulous place for someone who loves hills. For two days, he was completely alone with his solitude. He spent those two days sitting by the lake, and at night, he saw the reflection of that small town on the dark and calm surface of lake. It seemed as if the sky has come down in the valley in a compressed and small form with all its bright stars.

The stars that are no longer visible to people living in big polluted cities, glow and twinkle in their full glamour for people staying up in the hills away from the world and all its hulla-bulla. He stayed in a hotel by the lakeside and the window of his room overlooked the lake. He missed Devyani every moment and committed that someday he will bring her along with him, and that they will share every moment of beauty together.

It was tough getting back to Lucknow after such a beautiful and brief stay, but life has to go on, and one needs to attend dutifully whatever life calls in for. It was warm in Lucknow. Late autumn, dry winds, trees without leaves and dusty mornings all set an ideal stage for a melancholy odyssey.

Divaker started executing his new plans. He opened a current account in the name of his firm, designed a logo himself on CorelDraw advanced software, and got letterheads, visiting cards and bill book printed. He also applied for a service tax registration, consulted a chartered accountant and so on.........

He also gave a newspaper ad:

"Wanted Tata Indica/Maruti Van/ Maruti Esteem on short and long term lease. Vehicles in good condition required. Good returns assured. Only owners having commercial registration need to contact."

Around fifteen-twenty people responded to the advertisement. Out of them, he short listed five and called them to meet.

His game plan was to take cars from these people on lease for fixed amount every month. Fuel and driver cost would be borne by him, and regular maintenance had to taken care of by the vehicle owner. In case of any accident or major expenditure, insurance claim has to be made, but to keep things going, the matter has to be resolved by mutual co-operation. He made a lease agreement with all the clause and sub clauses.

To begin with, Divaker fixed upon a Tata Indica car, and a Maruti Van. He already had few contacts from his exposure to the pharma industry, and they started giving him business from day one. The equation that he had worked upon seemed successful. Both the cars began eating miles and produced some silver. He started making some money, which although was nothing significant, but then, it was definitely the money earned out of something that belonged entirely to him. The average running cost of a diesel car is approx four rupees per km – cost of fuel and driver included. He saved two rupees per km. On an average, the odometer clocked in between five and six thousand kms per month. After paying the vehicle owner their due share, he was left with around three-four thousand rupees per car, multiplied by two cars.

However, there were loopholes in his formula, which came to notice after some time. He did not take into consideration the credit factor, cost of fuel burned to collect payments, cost of phone, stationary etc. He realized that to keep himself afloat he required to increase the fleet. He took up two more cars on lease and started making new customers. But, when he increased the numbers of car, he lost control over the system. Now he required more hands to handle the system, but his resources did not allow hiring a full time guy to assist him.

Suddenly, an idea flashed in his mind. Why not ask Papa to come and join hands. Government had closed down the department for which Papa worked, and they were forced to take voluntary retirement. He was doing nothing back in the small village in a unanimous remote district of West Bengal. He was hopping from place to place savoring the hospitality of relatives, who had very high regards for him on his face, but laughed and made fun on his back – and Papa never understood it.

'Ha ha ha......, this is what they call a gazetted officer.'

'Whole life in towns and cities, and now back to dung.'

'Elephants teeth, different ones to show and different ones to eat.'

'Not even a single piece of land, this man, huh........'

Divaker wanted him to get out of that rut. He did not want him to lose his fake dignity and respect that he had earned throughout his life at an old age, only because he had no significant success in his life, monetary or otherwise. Papa was back from his posting in Assam, after retirement. Misty was in a boarding school. He could not buy a piece of land in his lifetime, not even a small flat. He had spent all his income for his kids and the impoverished and malnourished family in village, Divaker's chacha, Bua, Dada, Dadi etc etc.....

Papa had nothing left with him except some P.F and gratuity funds, an old carpet, glass tabletop, sofa, termite ridden bed and stuff like mixer-grinder, TV, fridge etc. Within a month of arrival in the village, a lightning hit the TV antenna, and voltage fluctuation blew up the fridge compressor. Termites wrote a chapter in history called 'The fall of the Bed' and the carpet became a culture medium for different kinds of moss, fungus and other microbes.

Divaker wanted to take him out of this humiliation. A man without a shelter of his own is like a street dog – this may sound rude but most of the truths are not pleasant. He offered Papa a proposition that would have worked out positively for both of them. One evening he discussed it with him over dinner. Papa had come to stay with Divaker for a fortnight.

'I don't feel like starting anything all over again. I am just whiling away time these days, waiting for my end to come. I won't be able to manage these things. I don't want to learn new things. After being ditched by your Maa, I have lost trust in everyone else. I am here for few days and then I will go back to my village. I have some money left, and I can pass the rest of my life somehow. I don't want to be a burden on you or anyone else,' Papa said.

'You won't be a burden on me. What I am talking about is doing something together, where we both will take care and bring up the business. After all, life does not end after retirement. People do some part time job. It's not about money only, lots of them just do social service,' Divaker said.

Papa finished the dinner and walked over to the sink to wash hands. He took out a matchstick and started using it as a toothpick. Divaker was wondering how to initiate the discussion again, as Papa pretended having heard nothing.

'Tomatoes are bit expensive here in Lucknow,' Papa said after sometime, trying to deviate the topic.

Divaker did not respond to his comment and brought the topic back on track.

'Leave aside taking care and handling business. Ok, that's fine with me. I will manage. I just want to know whether you are willing to stay with me or will you be going back to village?' he asked.

'I told you, I won't be a burden on anyone. I will go back to my village,' Papa said, and walked out of the room on the open roof and started puffing a cigarette.

Papa stayed for a month and then went back to village. While going back, on way to the railway station, he again hurt Divaker.

'Today you are asking me to stay. What security do I have? Tomorrow you will ask me to leave. Yesterday, you were doing a job, today you are running taxi, and tomorrow God knows what you will do. How can I entrust my life on you?'

Divaker did not say anything. The train arrived an hour late. He helped Papa board the train and arranged his luggage properly. The train moved put of the platform, and he walked out of the station thinking about all that Papa had said:

'Take care of yourself.'

'Sleep early, wake up early too.'

'Take lots of fruits and green vegetables.'

'Have your meals on time.'

'Yesterday you.......today.......tomorrow'

'How can I entrust..........?'

He had to bring down the scale of operations due to lack of resources – finance and manpower. He did not have enough money to keep the show running and meanwhile keep on bleeding financially.

One ill-fated evening he got a call from Jaipur that Misty was admitted in ICU. The Hostel warden had called up.

'She met with an accident. She and her friend, on way to the market on their scooty, please come as early as possible. Her parents could not be contacted,' the warden said and hung up.

Divaker had twenty thousand in his bank account. He withdrew all of it from an ATM and boarded the next flight. Papa and Maa arrived next day; they came to know when a messenger from the nearest town went to the village. Misty was out of danger by the time they reached. Divaker stayed there for four days. Misty was discharged from the ICU, but she had to stay in general ward for few more days. Maa and Papa planned to stay for another few days.

Back in Lucknow, the state of affairs further worsened. Few of his customers were upset having not received the services as expected. They got hold of some other taxi operator. Things were running out of control and his finances hit an all time low. He desperately needed some miraculous intervention or he wouldn't have enough money even for meals. The lease payoff dates seemed to knock quite early that month. He had no money to payoff the car owners. The landline phone's outgoing calls were barred due to non-payment.

An angel came to his rescue in the form of a job consultant.

'There's an opening in a FMCG company at Lucknow. Would you be interested?' the voice on the other side of the phone asked. It was music to his ears, and all he could gather was:

'Sure, yes, sure.'

Divaker did not even ask what package, what company and from where they got his cell number. A couple of days went by and no contact from their side. He called back on the number from which the call had come.

'Sure Sir, we will let you know as soon as we get a confirmation from the employer to go ahead with the selection process,' a polite lady said.

'Well, fine. Can you give me some idea about the salary package, and the company?' Divaker asked, thinking that it's better to get few answers meanwhile.

She told him that the consultancy firm got his resume from Naukri.com – a job placement website – on which Divaker had once registered free of cost. This was a reputed company in Fast Moving Consumer Goods segment, and they were ready to give up to twenty percent hike on the existing package.

A week went by, and nothing happened. Divaker had no idea of what was going to happen next. From four cars, his business had shrunk to only one car which most of the time was parked outside the gate and the driver played cricket with neighborhood boys. He left everything for God to decide and fix up for him.

'I told you not to quit the job,' Devyani said.

'I know, but then it's not a sin to try and experiment new things in life. At least, I had the courage to move out of the box, which most people do not have,' he then gave her a long lecture on the morale of a short and powerful book, which was a tale of four rats and their story of cheese.

One day his phone rang, and the display blinked.

'CONSULTANT, CONSULTANT, CONSULTANT.....'

'Mr. Divaker?'

'Yes.'

'The company has fixed up interviews next Wednesday. Shall I ask them to send the tickets or will you buy them on your own, however in case of latter, the tickets will be reimbursed on the spot.'

'No, no, please. Please ask them to send the tickets by courier,' every single rupee was important to him, and he did not want to part with a single piece of it. He was already running on reserve fund.

Ten days later, he was on the payroll of a famous FMCG company.

Divaker handed over the last car to its owner and settled the balance lease amount. He also paid off the landline bill and got outgoing calling facility activated, all from the imprest cash that he received at the time of joining that company.

One and a half year after joining this company, he married Devyani. It was not a grand ceremony. Few months before the marriage he left his 'small love nest' and moved into a larger flat – with two bedrooms and a drawing dining space – in a different locality. He also started buying household things like TV, fridge, utensils, almirah etc.

Another year in Lucknow, he got a promotion. The long awaited promotion at last arrived. He had started earning well. Devyani had completed her masters degree, and meanwhile got selected for the banking job. They were both doing well in their careers and the household income was enough to lead a respectable and good lifestyle. On weekends, they visited Uncle and Aunty. It was only half an hour drive from their place. Divaker's parents also visited them after every few months but had no plans to stay permanently. Once when Maa came to visit, he asked her one day:

'You always asked me that, when am I going to bring you along to stay with me. Things are almost in place now. What do you plan next Maa?'

'Not this year. I have certain things and duties to pay-off. But yes, this is the only place I can always take shelter. I will come, but not now,' she replied, looking at an empty corner of the living room

Maa was an unfortunate human being. God knows what kind of destiny He had written for her. She was one of nine brothers and sisters in her family. Her father was a teacher, and had lot of property that came to him automatically after marriage with Naniji.

The upbringing of nine children in a far-flung village can well be imagined. They were a well to do family; they had no shortage of food, and they got some kind of education also, at least up to basic school which was run by Nanaji. Then, at an early age, she was married to Papa. Papa qualified for the marriage only because he was in a good job, otherwise there was a big cultural and economic gap in both the families, and a big age difference between Maa and Papa. She had come with lots of hopes and expectations from her husband and the new relationship – things that she had heard from her other married sisters, but Papa was so busy supporting and feeding his own family back in the village, that he was not able to rise up to her needs and expectations.

She also could not fit in the scenario that was thrown in front of her, and on which she had no control. Papa had to support two families at a time, 'us' and 'they'.

Education of his younger brother.

Marriage of his sisters.

Money to repair the leaking roof that leaked during monsoons.

Money to purchase agricultural land.

Clothes for all during festivals and ceremonies.

Medicines when somebody was ill.

Cost of installing a new tube well.

Etc…etc…etc……

They dominated and controlled everything in Divaker's family. Papa bought a refrigerator when Divker was a kid. Dadaji had come over to their place to get a health check up done and take some cash back along with him.

'What was the use of buying this? Such a waste of money only for cold water,' Dadaji said in front of everybody.

Papa was posted in a small town of U.P called Jhansi that time. Papa did not buy him a toy or even an ice cream while Dadaji stayed with them. Divaker felt bad about it and when Dadaji finally left, Divaker saw him tucking a pad of currency in a hidden pocket of pyjama somewhere near the groin.

14

Vidyapeeth

Since childhood, Divaker never saw Papa and Maa living a healthy and happy married life. They always quarreled and fought over issues, which he did not understand that time, but now he understands everything. Misty was born when they were in Jhansi.

From Jhansi, Papa was transferred to Allahabad. Their acquaintance with Devyani and her family started there. Divaker was entering his teen years. He was twelve years old, and then another turning point came in his life. He had to go to a boarding school in Bihar. Maa fought for it. She perhaps knew that all their turmoil would have a long lasting impact on him. He was sent to the boarding school and was soon forgotten, except for a postcard in between vacation, and sometimes not even that. It was only during the summer vacation that he used to go home – Allahabad.

Remember................

'Two months of vacation every year, for four years.'

A totally different facade of life revealed itself during the years at Vidyapeeth. The complete ownership of his character building, personality development, understanding of self-respect and integrity goes to Vidyapeeth and its environment. It was a disciplined boy's school up to secondary level. They had to wake up at 5:30 am,

Exercise, and Yoga,

Breakfast and classes,

Lunch and washing own plates, bowls etc,

Afternoon rest,

Football and prayer,

Dinner, and then washing your own plates, bowls etc.

Sunday it was a different routine for the first half of the day.

Haircut – compulsory for anyone having hairs more than an inch.

Polishing shoes, cleaning the hostel.

Working at the football field.

Learning music or reading books etc.

Lunch and the washing your own plates, bowls etc.

Rest of the day was as usual. Swamiji's, who were devoted to Lord Ramakrishna and Swami Vivekananda, ran the school. Being disciples of Swami Vivekananda, they were all pledged to never marry, and lead a single life, dedicated to God, social service and humanity. Swami Vivekananda established the Vidyapeeth with an objective and vision of creating a generation of young men who would have strength of will, power of knowledge, love for humanity, sanctity of character, and unquestionable levels of integrity.

Divaker personally, even to this day, believed in few basic and fundamental elements of whatever he had learnt at Vidyapeeth. They taught meditation, yoga and the power of thinking. Ways to control mind and focus its energy. The people, environment and tough life at Vidyapeeth inspired him. He understood the feeling of taking bath at 5:30 am in winters. Catching an afternoon sleep in dormitory under a tin roof that too in peak summers when the temperature soared up to 47 degrees, and eating chapattis which tasted salty, with the sweat of workers making them at a coal furnace for hours at one go. Life was not easy, but that was the time, which laid the foundation stone for rest of his life.

Brief holidays had nothing to do with him, as his parents never visited him nor did they ever send instructions to the student council office to arrange for his travel. Often on mid term vacations, he along with half a dozen boys stayed back in the hostel, whereas hundreds of other inmates went back to their homes.

Divaker absorbed the essence of Vidyapeeth in such a way that at a point of time he decided not to marry in his life.

He was just a kid then.

A grown up kid.

Divaker tried his hand at violin, singing and drama. He also played football for the school team at district level. He was the sub-editor of quarterly wall magazine. He understood the power of truth and integrity, and realized that it was a tough option to choose amongst other lucrative options that are always up for sale a much lower price. Along with these values, he also had some idea about homosexuality. They did not teach about it, but in a confined area of single sex population, nothing more innovative could have ever sprung up from the masculine football grounds, which had tasted more male sweat than monsoon rain.

'Talking of values' and 'walking on values' are two different things. Its not that he always walked on values, it's a battlefield out there, in this wide open world, where everyone is consistently fighting for survival, lust, money and greed. To survive and thrive in this battlefield, one needs to know the tricks of the game. Divaker learnt those tricks the hard way round – knocking doors, selling detergents, negotiating on values, compromising on every breath he inhaled, and swallowing down the bitter and pungent aftertaste, thereafter. But, it felt bad and disgusting every time, as if someone had stripped him at a bazaar and made him run naked with a candle stuck up in his ass. Spectators all round him laughing, howling, and pointing at his genitals. It felt that bad.

But, only if one has something inside, which makes one feel, react, form notions and think twice about it.

Otherwise, it's just another day in the market, brisk business and regular trading going on.

Some months back Divaker and a business associate went to a missionary hospital for some tender purchase related issues. In our country, nothing is sorted out until and unless smiling Gandhiji comes to rescue from green currency notes. The same thing was about to happen, he knew very well. Doing business is becoming tough day by day, profit margins reducing, increasing credit period, concern about quality etc etc etc. The customer wants everything. He listened to all the blah blah blah from his associate.

The key person of the tender committee appeared in the parking lot. Divaker's associate had a talk with him, and he slipped a white envelope in the deep pockets of the saffron robe, which the person was wearing. The associate had asked Divaker to stay a little away from the dealing, as the other person would not have preferred the presence of a 'third party' in his deal. Divaker's associate came back running to him when the other person had vanished, and said a lot of things in very less time, only this could be understood -

'Job done! Job done! We will be getting it!'

The other person did not recognize Divaker, but Divaker

recognized him. He was one of his teachers in Vidyapeeth.

The years at Vidyapeeth were totally alienated from what happened back at home. He just used to get a 'passer-by' view of the situation, whenever he was there on vacations. The situation was becoming more and more violent. It seemed as if they no longer wanted to see each other's face, or live a single moment together.

During his last year at Vidyapeeth, he went to Nanaji's place to spend summer vacation. Maa and Misty were along with him. Papa called up one day and informed that he has been transferred to Assam. He said he would be moving in a week's time. Divaker felt bad as he knew that perhaps he won't be able to meet his friends back at Allahabad. In addition, he won't be able to meet Devyani anymore.

A fortnight later Papa informed that he has shifted to Assam, and that he was coming to meet Divaker and Misty. Divaker had no idea that a storm was brewing up, and the same storm would disrupt their life forever. Papa arrived the next day and then the events happened in such a quick succession that it was not possible for Divaker to differentiate one from another. It was like a fast forward video tape.

Papa created a big scene in front of the whole village.

He said that Maa is a characterless woman.

He said he had proofs, like letters.

He said that Maa had an extra-marital affair with their landlord in Allahabad.

He wanted to take Misty along with him.

He did not want Maa to enter back in his life, ever.

If Misty would not be 'given' to him, he threatened to give a divorce.

He also said that Maa, and her illegitimate ally had planned to murder him.

The whole village watched them; Nanaji was speechless and did not know how to react. Misty was only eight years old. She held the saree of Maa and started howling and weeping. Divaker felt as if a huge monster had appeared out of nowhere and his legs were rooted to the ground. He wanted to escape but he could not. The whole village watched them. It was something more than mere humiliation.

It was death of respect for Divaker and the family, a disgusting tattoo right on their forehead, for whole life to carry and announce a disgraceful past.

Divaker had no idea who was right or who was wrong. Even today, he doesn't know what exactly happened. That day elders in the family agreed that it's better to 'give' Misty to Papa rather than having a divorce. Moreover, if Misty stays with her father, her future would be more secure. Divaker wept, Maa wept, Misty sobbed and many women of the village started to weep, seeing the pathetic situation of their family. They were all watching a live family drama, a live version of the tragic part of a run-of-the-mill evening soap on TV.

It had been raining for the last few days, making the paddy fields greener. The sun shone more brightly making the weather hot and humid. It was late afternoon.

Misty was wearing a torn cotton frock, and Divaker was wearing a pajama. They took whatever clothes Maa collected in a hurry, and put them in a polythene bag. Both of them started off with Papa on the moped that Papa had borrowed from someone to reach the venue of this event. Maa was in a shock and she had stopped weeping. She did not talk when they left, and simply watched them. Misty had a sore throat that choked with her howling and weeping. All she could say in a croaking voice was:

'Maa, Maa, Maa.....Dada, Dada.........ummm....Maaaa, Da....... Da...ummmm......'

It was very agonizing to think about these entire disturbances from her point of view, from the point of view of an eight-year-old girl. They were suffering for something they did not do, and had no control over. The moped jumped and bumped over the muddy potholes of village road. Around a hundred people came to see them off. Some of them comforted Maa, some comforted Nanaji, who was also shocked, defeated and humiliated.

The group of people became smaller and smaller as the moped moved away from them, on the muddy road by the side of river. Divaker turned back to see them, but they were no longer visible. They had taken a turn on the winding country road. Misty was so exhausted that she slept leaning on Divaker, her mouth open. Divaker held her strongly so that she does not fall off from the tiny vehicle. All the way tears kept on running from his eyes. He cursed everything and everyone. He was fifteen, but he had felt the agony of a lifetime that day. Papa's village was ten miles away from Nanaji's place. It was dark when they reached.

Divaker went back to hostel when the holidays were over, and Misty went back with Papa to the new place of posting, a small town in lower Assam. Life started all over again, like a tornado hit area. Divaker had to prepare for the board exams, which was only six months ahead. Misty was admitted to a good convent school. Maa had nothing to do except increase Nanaji's expenses. In the beginning, nobody had problems but then slowly, the presence of a married woman staying with her parents started creating problems. She was fortunate to get a part time teaching job in a primary school. The salary was peanuts – Rupees 800 per month but then she at least had something, and she started earning enough to meet her personal expenses. This way Maa separated from Divaker and Misty. She always said,

'Grow up early Beta and stand tall on your feet. Someday take me out of this place with honor and respect. I will feel that the disgraceful way in which your Papa abandoned me has been compensated.'

However, gradually she adjusted into her habitat. After some years, she got a full time job and her salary increased to twenty five hundred per month. Nanaji gave her a piece of property and she started making some more money out of lending that property on lease.

That was her part of the story. She still lives in her village and she visits Divaker twice every year. She has no plans of coming back permanently to stay with him. Once bitten twice shy. She did not intend to put all her eggs in the same basket. The eggs had all been broken once.

Misty stayed with Papa, and completed her schooling in Assam. Then she appeared in an entrance test for a course in management. She qualified and moved to Jaipur. She stayed in a hostel and pursued her studies. With nothing called a 'home,' during vacations and holidays, she often came down to Lucknow. Divaker had a nice time with her. They understood each other well, because they both had been through same experiences in past.

After Vidyapeeth, Divaker moved over to a different school in Ranchi – a city in southern Bihar – for senior secondary studies. He wanted to be a doctor, he had secured ninety percent in science, but indecision and lack of guidance pushed him to do what he saw his friends doing. He pursued studies in commerce.

Once, Divaker called up Mishra Uncle's old number in Allahabad from a STD booth and came to know that a lot of noise and rumors was spread around, when Papa left Allahabad. Everybody had a different story to say. Divaker thanked God that he was not there at that time. From whatever Aunty said, he understood that their family had earned a notorious reputation, before Papa left Allahabad, and took a long distance transfer to Assam. The wounds had not healed up, and he did not call them up again.

From Ranchi he passed the senior secondary exams with average results, and headed straight for Delhi. From a brilliant student he declined to levels of mediocrity. Divaker started his real life from Delhi and gradually, slowly and slowly the wound healed up. Remember.............

Correspondence course

Salesman job

Lot of those jobs

Friendship with Gaurav

Completion of his grads degree

Going back to Assam

The job in that multinational company

Meerut

Arif's marriage, Allahabad again

Devyani

Her medical entrance exam in Meerut

Chatting over phone

He proposed

She accepted

Long distance romance

Valentine Day

Transfer to Lucknow

Job dissatisfaction

Resignation

Starting up car rental business

Closing down car rental business

Another job opportunity

Marriage

His promotion and Devyani's job in the bank

A well settled life, touchwood............

Life, as they say, could be summarized in a single word, and sometimes cannot be defined in a whole book. Divaker was at halfway point of life. He had traveled, and needs to travel almost the same distance more. Divaker did not see tomorrow, it may happen that the another half is only as brief as a single day or a week, a month, a year or a few years. But, we all think as if this life would never end, a journey, where the traveler is not prepared or intent on arriving. A man travels, fails, gains, learns, teaches, falls, succeeds and then again keeps going.

He liked a brand of whiskey. The label said:

'Keep Walking'

Divaker had given up drinking a long time back.

14

The Transfer

'Good things don't stay in life for long.'

Is it a philosophy?

A negative way of interpreting things and events?

The voice of an insecure soul?

Or just,

Practical experiences of someone who said it.

Divaker does not know, but this thing proved to be hundred percent true in his case. When everything was just at the corner of being perfect, the power of destiny had again thrown bits of the puzzle game. Divaker sat down again on the floor, collected all the pieces and started matching them, corner-to-corner, observing whether the face of a lion or an elephant or Mickey Mouse may appear out of those pieces.

A year back. A year back from tonight, almost, he was transferred to Delhi. The guy posted in Delhi had resigned, and Divaker's boss referred Divaker to fill in the vacancy.

'You will boil like a frog,' he said, 'you have been here in Lucknow for very long. If tomorrow we need to promote you further, the first thing that company will see is, whether you have an experience of metro market or not. Work here for a year or so, and wait for your next career elevation. Yes, you need to keep performing, just the way you are doing a good job in Lucknow.'

'Ok Sir, whatever you think would be better for me,' he said.

He did not tell his boss that he had heard the same story earlier also, some years back, and trusted the person who told it. He did not tell him the profit and loss of similar move some years back. A thunder is not always followed by rains, and rains are not always followed by rainbow.

He discussed it with Devyani. At that point, it was real tough call for both of them to take.

'What do you feel about this?' Devyani asked.

'Means?'

'Do you see the benefit of this move? Do you feel it will help you in some way in your career?' she asked.

'Yes, if ever the question of my promotion comes across, this will be the first pre requisite to qualify for even the eligibility criteria,' he replied.

'Hmmmm......'

'What's really troubling me is the change. I had planned to settle down in Lucknow. I don't like Delhi. I am sick of that city,' he told her the issue honestly.

Mentally, she was stronger than Divaker. She could take tough and unpleasant decisions.

'Then what about my job?' she asked.

'Well, ummm.... I don't want you to quit. Nobody gets a good job easily these days. In addition, nobody has seen what tomorrow has in store for us. A job means a lot of security. There is no fun taking up a job, doing it for a year and then suddenly quitting it.'

'Yeah true, even I don't want to quit.'

'But, if say, I need you in Delhi and I ask you to leave your job, then?'

She laughed and Divaker laughed. He knew that she would never quit, and she also knew what Divaker knew. Unspoken understandings.

'Better talk to them, and put down an application for transfer to Delhi. Whenever there is a vacancy, they will shift you. Isn't it?' he asked.

'Yes, that's how it should happen ideally, but there are so many transfer applications already in waiting that I wonder when is that going to happen.'

Life is never perfect. We keep on hoping that maybe the next turn and things would change, things will be perfect, things would become as we always dream, but then nothing happens, or sometimes they happen in the most unexpected way. We then wait for the next corner, the next bend, the next crossroad and keep hoping.

Divaker had to take charge in fifteen days. He went Delhi. His colleague helped him get an accommodation. House rent in Delhi is ridiculous for a person who comes from a non-metro city. It was again a one-room portion, with kitchen and attached toilet. The locality was somewhat good. Rupees 4500 per month.

He had to give three months advance rent and finalize the things. He then went back to Lucknow to bring in clothes and stuff which he would need everyday:

Toaster

Pressure cooker

Blankets

Some basic utensils

Bike

And a lot of other knick-knacks

There was no need of the rented house in Lucknow anymore. Devyani went back to stay with her parents. They packed up all the things that he did not want to carry and she had no use at her parents place, and kept those things in a room upstairs at Mishra Uncle's place, all packed up.

'Someday we will take these things back when we again start living together,' Divaker said.

He saw their household things for the last time, put a padlock in the room and handed over the keys to Devyani. He wanted to cry like a child.

He was again going to lead a single life, far away from her. He was alone all over again. He had no one in this world except her. Often it came to his mind that he should ask Devyani to leave her job, and come over to Delhi. He did not. He did not want to prune her career and self-reliance only for his benefit; moreover, he knew that it was never going to happen.

He thought:

'Where would she go?'

'What would she do?'

'What would happen to our kids?'

'If one day, I suddenly die leaving everything. I do not have enough wealth to last for even a single year. A lifetime is much longer,'

None of Devyani's sisters ever felt the need of taking care of parents. After marriage, everyone created a world of his or her own. Uncle and Aunty had nobody to buy medicines if they ever fall ill.

Divakers parents lived in joint families of their own. On papa's side, he had:

Two younger brothers, both married, and their kids of all ages, starting from three months to eight years. He was not lonely. He played with the kids, bought vegetables for the family from evening village bazaar, watched TV all day, boozed in the evening and updated his bank statement from time to time.

On Maa's side, she had:

Nanaji and Naniji, three brothers, one unmarried and two married with many kids. In addition, she also had a job that kept her busy most of the time.

After the separation, all of them in their small family lost something called 'oneness.' Nobody is to be blamed for it. After all, lesser mortals do not plan or control everything. His parents did not take a divorce but the arrangement was perhaps worse than a divorce, something like an 'emotional constipation' – he heard this word in a movie featuring animated elephant, zebra, lion, giraffe and lots of lemur like creature.

All of them in his family had a life of their own, a circle of their own, with no overlapping. One thing was certain. All of them were happy in their own worlds, with occasional pangs of frustration, despair and depression. Misty and Divaker felt the same way. Maa and Papa also felt the same, or maybe everyone pretended to feel that way. Their family started meeting again like an alumni association, when Divaker was in Lucknow. It was once a year event. They did not talk on matters of common agreement or disagreement but rather had tales from their own 'land'.

They were no longer interested in things like:

The design of dining table

Which flower to grow this winter

None of them had anything to poke their nose into anyone else's matter.

Maa and Papa had developed expertise over how to avoid topics that involved some kind of responsibility and liability. Matters like-

Divaker's marriage

Misty's Marriage

A much-needed computer for Misty

A house or a piece of land for Divaker

Later, much later, in her last year of the management course, everybody came to know that Misty had married a guy of the same college, one year senior to her.

No ceremonies, no dinner, nothing, only signatures at the marriage registrar office. Maa and Papa reacted as if something grossly illegitimate had all of a sudden happened. Divaker did not react, and asked them to have patience. Divaker was fortunate that the girl who entered his life was daughter of his parent's friend belonging to same caste. They obviously did not find any issues with his marriage. However, had it not been Devyani, then it would have been someone else, and that necessarily would not have amused his parents much. Divaker was okay with Misty's marriage.

'When you have nothing, you shouldn't be afraid of losing anything.'

Divaker heard many times that child of broken family end up as failure. However, contrary to this, both Divaker and Misty were doing pretty fine in their own lives. He was almost well settled, and she did wonderful in all her exams. She had a career once she is over with the course.

With the type of upbringing and environment their parents gave, they should not be expecting anything in return except for the support in their old age, when they would have nothing left in their hands. They should not be expecting smaller things in life, which does not although change the picture but yes, it lends beauty and charm, smaller strokes of varied colors.

He informed both Papa and Maa regarding his transfer.

'It would be more difficult now,' Papa said.

'Yes, but not that much, only five hundred kilometers from Lucknow,' he said.

'That means one more night in the train?'

'Yes, almost.'

Maa was bothered because Devyani was staying back in Lucknow.

'She could have come along with you,' Maa said.

'Yes.....but........'

'What but? Is job more important or a married life, especially for a woman? She can find a job in Delhi also,' Maa interrupted in between.

Divaker did not waste much time in giving her a full understanding of unemployment rate in the country, nor did he discuss any of his own problems and limitations.

He felt like asking:

'Maa, why don't you quit your own job and stay with your son? After all, he would be staying all alone with nobody to cook and take care. He may need your help.'

He did not however say anything like this. It's bad pricking healed up wounds.

Divaker had packed in almost everything required for his 'camp' in Delhi. Both Divaker and Devyani felt as if the end of everything had come.

They wanted to say many things to each other

They wanted to hug each other tightly and say nothing.

He wanted to kiss her passionately.

They wanted to weep, holding each other.

He wanted to whisper softly in her ear, 'I love you.'

They wanted to do a lot of things but the situation and environment did not allow. Divaker's heart wanted a lot of things, but his body and mind were not aligned.

Aunty came in the room with a pack of mosquito repellant and naphthalene balls. She said,

'On weekends try coming over to Lucknow. It's only with your support that we are able to see a future for ourselves, before we die, or else we old people have nobody.'

She started sobbing, and wiping her tears with the corner of her dupatta.

'Mummy, please don't....,' Devyani shouted, irritated.

Divaker did not know what he should say to make her feel better. He however managed to say:

'Please don't worry. Devyani is here. She is a responsible young lady. She is no longer a child na? I will be coming here most of the weekends, and Delhi is not a far off place. It's just seven-eight hours by train.'

At ten o' clock at night, the train was scheduled. He had a light dinner with them. Uncle did not say anything throughout. They silently left the table one by one. He still had two hours. They were having coffee.

'Everything that belongs to me also belongs to Devyani and

you. You are more of a son, rather than a son-in-law. Take care of yourself and see if you can again come back to lucknow,' Uncle said at last.

'Yes, I know that Uncle,' Divaker said.

All three of them came to see him off at their small gate. Perhaps Devyani wanted to say something, but could not say in their presence.

Divaker took a riksha and went to the main road, where he got a cab. He reached railway station on time and saw the Delhi bound 'Lucknow Mail' waiting on platform. He searched for his berth and tucked away the two bags and a carton full of his 'camping material' under the berth. He stretched on the berth, and immediately the phone started ringing. It was Devyani's call. She was silent for some time.

'You reached station?' she asked.

'Yes, just five minutes back.'

'I wanted to talk to you about something.....'

'Yes, I know, but we could not, everybody was around.'

'We were planning to conceive......'

He had no answers. He felt helpless. She had pricked in a needle right on a wound that had been giving him pain since the time of transfer. In fact, he was so helpless with the matter that he did not have courage to talk about it. It was a sensitive issue for both of them and maybe that is the reason she kept on procrastinating it, but finally the ice had been broken.

'Yes true. Only since last month we had been trying.'

'Yes, I stopped taking contraceptives from 15th, the day we went to the Doctor.'

'See, if something is already fixed up, we can't help. We need to welcome our baby with whatever best possible way we can.

You will have to go on maternity leave. This time we will never do what we did before marriage. Never ever.'

'Yes, I agree with you Divaker,' she said.

'During those crucial days, if in case it happens, I will be with you as much as possible. No need to take the contraceptives anymore, as we won't be sleeping together every night. Lastly, if anything is there, the symptoms will tell you this month only. Let's wait and see.'

'Ok,' she said, 'what if nothing happens?'

'If nothing happens, well and good, we will plan out once we are settled over this thing, this transfer and dislocation thing, okay?'

'Ok.'

They said nothing to each other for some time. A brief and strange silence prevailed between them. The train started to move. Inside an AC compartment, especially at night, it's only a slight pull that tells that the train has started to move.

'The train has pulled off,' he said breaking the momentary silence between the two of them.

'So, we are not going to have a baby?' she asked abruptly.

'I never said this thing Devyani. I never said that we are not going to have a baby. It's only a matter of time. We planned something and it did not work out. We still have some chances, who knows. Maybe our baby has already set foot in this world. Just wait and let's see what happens. I will hug you, and give you a dozen kisses if you say that you have conceived. The only thing I want to say is that lets not go ahead with our planning anymore in the present scenario. It's got to be tough, for both of us. Are you getting me sweetheart?'

'Yes, I understand. I will pray, and ask God to make things a bit smooth for both of us.'

'Sure my, love, things will be okay soon. Take care of yourself, Uncle and Aunty. Also, eat properly and don't take too much stress. I will always be somewhere around you. You only need to think about me, and miss me,' Divaker said, and he meant every word of what he had said.

'You too take care. Get a local cellular connection, first thing after you reach Delhi. We can't talk much in roaming mode.'

'Definitely my love, sleep early tonight, you've got office tomorrow. Good night.'

'Good night.'

Divaker did not sleep, he was thinking about a lot of things with eyes wide open. He did not know when he rolled into sleep on that narrow berth of train compartment, and saw a recurrent dream.

Flood waters everywhere, a small town or maybe a village, no name, and a deserted railway station. He is waiting for a train and its drizzling. The sky is dark and overcast. It's very cold and gloomy. The wind carried those flaky water droplets randomly. The drizzle brought down with it more darkness. It's already evening and the world was getting more and more dark. Divaker saw a man coming towards him with a lantern in hand. He came close to him. He was a frail old man, with a plastic cement bag wrapped around him to keep off the rain, but he was dripping wet. Divaker asked that old man that when will the train arrive, and the man said that the train had already gone yesterday, no train today.

He opened his eyes and saw Devyani sleeping beside him. He has to leave for Delhi today.

"No, I understand. I will pray and ask God to make things [illegible] for both of us."

"Sure my love, things will be okay soon. Take care of yourself [illegible] and [illegible]. Also eat properly and don't take too much stress. I will always be somewhere around you. You only need to think about me, and I miss [illegible]," Dhruba said, and he meant every word of what he had said.

"You too take care. [illegible] a local cellular connection, first thing after you reach Delhi. We can't talk much in roaming mode."

"[illegible] my love, sleep early tonight. You've got office tomorrow. Good night."

"Good night."

Dhruba did not sleep; he was thinking about a lot of things [illegible] eyes wide open. He did not know when he rolled into sleep on the narrow berth of train compartment and saw a recurrent dream.

[illegible] covers everywhere, a small town or maybe a village, [illegible] and a deserted railway station. He is waiting for a train and it [illegible]. The sky is dark and overcast. It's [illegible] cold and gloomy. The wind carried tiny little water droplets [illegible]. The [illegible] brought [illegible]. It's already evening and the [illegible] was getting more and more dark. Dhruba saw a man coming towards him with a lantern in hand. He came close to him. He was a frail old man with a [illegible] wrapped around him [illegible], but he was [illegible]. Dhruba asked the old man when will the train come, and the man said that the train had already gone yesterday, no train today.

He opened his eyes and saw [illegible] sleeping beside him. He has to leave for Delhi today.

15

..... Back

It's almost the same morning as yesterday, same winter sun, same terrace and almost the same weather.

Yesterday he was happy

Today he is not

Yesterday he had 'today' with him

Today he does not have any other tomorrow

He has to leave tonight by Lucknow Mail.

Devyani woke up early. Early means immediately after he sat by her side, brushed her hair, kissed her on the forehead and eyelids. He then opened the door to let some fresh air enter. He then went to the terrace to have a look at the day.

Divaker had always made her feel the most loved person in this world. Yes, they quarreled a lot like cats and dogs, but then their fights never turned into a permanent state of bitterness. Today, she owns the majority stake in their partnership and she deserved it. She is more functional in holding together the partnership and Divaker loved her passionately, more than his life, more than anything or anyone. She was fortunate that his love did not scatter among others. She took all of it, with all its bits and pieces.

'When did you wake up?' She asked, yawning and getting her hairs straight.

'Just few minutes back.'

'You had a good sleep?' she asked.

'Yes, sure, with my beloved in my arms it's obvious that I will get a sound sleep.'

'Wait I will get some tea,' she smiled and went downstairs.

Divaker brushed and washed his face. She appeared with cups and a teapot after some time. She looked fresh like a white orchid. A beam of white light reflecting from the house in front of their terrace came straight all the way through the door and washed her face.

'How is the tea?' she asked.

'Perfect Madam, as always.'

'Your return tickets are confirmed?' She asked.

'Yes, but I don't want to think about it now. I want to live every moment of our togetherness without worrying about any damn thing. So less time,' he said and pressed her hand.

'Why don't you come every weekend? At least we will be in regular touch, and I will have something to look forward to throughout the week. Isn't it possible some way?' she asked and looked into his eyes.

'It's not altogether impossible, but then I have so many things piled up, that sometime it's really impossible even to think about leaving Delhi. I don't have a computer in my room. I need to log in on Sundays from cyber café to fill up some format or compile data. I wash my clothes on Sundays. Often I need to do some shopping on Sundays, stuff like bread, eggs etc,' he briefly laughed, a hollow one, and then he continued, 'I drop my mobile bill cheque on Sundays. Petty small things that are not important, but definitely something you can't do without. But then, I squeeze out every minute possible and try to be here with you every two or three weeks.'

She listened to every word, and the expression on her face told that she visualized everything in her 'fertile' mind. Everything of what Divaker had said. After a pause she said,

'So, you have created a world of your own over there in Delhi? Isn't it?'

'Not exactly world, but a small camp, a base camp. It's a battle that I am fighting over there, for my family back at home.'

She was happy to hear this, her eyes brightened. She moved the cups, pot, and tray from the bed, jumped over Divaker and hugged him. She often behaved in a childish way and he wondered that how does she deal with everyday life. The word 'family' had perhaps triggered something in her mind.

She did not say anything but she was thinking about a new member in the family – a baby. Divaker was thinking about that too, but he kept quite. Perhaps avoiding things one can't help is the best possible way to resolve things – a philosophy that he had developed over past few years. To earn bread, he had to be in Delhi. Devyani was not capable enough to shoulder responsibility of a baby. Is it fair enough to bring in a new life, without caring enough for his upbringing? What possibly is the way out for them?

Or maybe, Divaker was not passionate enough to take that extra risk and walk that extra mile. There is no reason to do a thing, but numerous reasons for not doing it. He asked himself the same question and heard a hollow, sleepy, tired voice of resentment from inside. He had run short of energy and life. He did not have energy left in him to shoulder extra responsibilities, nor did he have the passion to do or die for the relationship.

The good old romance had vanished under thick wraps of dust and cobwebs, neglected and taken for granted.

God grant me the courage.......

To change things I can.......

The perseverance to.......

Accept things I can't.......

And the wisdom to know the difference.......

A very thin line separated the difference between things that can be changed, and things that cannot be changed. It takes a lifetime of wisdom to know the difference. The energy of youth says that everything can be changed. The experience of mid thirties and forties keeps dwindling between 'can' and 'cannot'. The wisdom of old age says that there are very few things that can be changed and human nature certainly does not fall in that category. Basic attitude and nature of a person remains unchanged, mostly.

Say, for example, Divaker had not been able to change few things in him, despite all efforts. His need for small things in life, love, and understanding remained unfulfilled. The insecurity phenomenon in his mind remained unchanged.

Things like:

She might be thinking about her past boyfriends, while going through old photo album.

What had they been doing when he suddenly entered the room and found her hand in hand with a boy – her distant cousin, laughing and giggling.

With whom she might be talking in whispers away in the terrace.

Small events of past somehow find their way in the present, and embed themselves in a way to create a picture, a perception, which is difficult to ignore, perhaps. Often he forgets all about it,

but mind, attitude and nature does not change every other day.

Divaker still hugged her, but his hands relaxed and loosened.

'What happened?' she asked.

'Nothing.'

'Something wrong again?'

'No, nothing. It's only that I need to leave tonight.'

'Try to come over next weekend too, will you?'

'I will try, let's see.'

She smiled and went downstairs to get breakfast. He took a quick shower. His head was dizzy and a mild headache irritated him. The shower helped him although.

He turned on the radio and sat on the terrace. It's the same type of weather as in Nainital, sharp sunshine and cool breeze. They had been there, right after marriage for honeymoon, a small hill station by the lake. He had fulfilled his dream of going back to Nainital a long time back with the person of his dreams. He was thinking of going back again for few days, alone.

He also remembered the quarrel, which they had on their second night of honeymoon over small matters like ignoring and overlooking his presence.

'You only need a husband to fulfill all your needs, feed you, and fuck you at night!'

A lot of damage had been done, injuries that never healed afterwards like a strained muscle of thigh that twitched at certain angles and movements.

Has she been able to ignore them all?

Has she forgotten all about those bitter moments?

Has she forgiven him?

Or,

Is everything still inside her heart?

Maybe, she also had swallowed the bitter potion of compromise and acceptance just like him.

Maybe, she is playing the 'pretender' game.

Or,

Has she already taken revenge against him, under the dark blanket of night? Squaring off everything even.

No, maybe not. Her eyes do not tell the story. It's actually the guilty conscious perhaps. She is also leading the same dull life of compromise and negotiation, probably. She was born to be a singer, a model, and she ended up being a bank clerk and a wife of an eternal insecure man. Divaker was born to be a poet, a writer, and he ended up as a salesman and husband of an insensitive woman. The romance, which was a part of lust and sultry needs, had vanished and now they were in terms to reality.

Does she think that way too?

'Breakfast is ready. Come downstairs,' she shouted from below the stairs.

Over the table, he looked at her innocent face and thought about the time when he was crazy for everything about her. It was 'deep love', and he was willing to do everything for her. Things have changed, gradually. He loves her deeply even today, especially on the bed, when his basic needs comes in close contact with the source of fulfillment.

He used to say:

'Love and lust are two different things.'

Yes, they are,

Two different things............

They love each other even today, after all the misunderstandings and gaps. However, the gaps existed.

Is it the same for everybody?

They had a reasonably good quality of life; they had almost everything a household needed and a good monthly income. Nobody from outside would ever imagine or guess about their problems, issues and concerns. Life went on like this for years and would continue for the rest of years in life.

After breakfast Divaker went to the bank to get a copy of bank statement and see the status of cheques issued for car loan, life insurance premium, mutual fund investment, and also his salary credit etc etc.

After lunch, he slept with Devyani.

In the evening, he packed up his bag for the return journey. He had a light dinner. The cab had arrived an hour before the scheduled train time.

'I will miss you miserably,' he said and kissed Devyani.

He moved out of their small flat, and the small gate. Uncle, Aunty and Devyani came up to the gate to see him off. He opened the door and sat inside the cab.

'Good bye, try to come next weekend.'

'Ok, sure. Hope I will.'

'Take care, and do call up everyday.'

'Talk to your boss and see if some transfer is possible back to Lucknow.'

'Give me a call when you reach there.'

The cab moved down the service lane before joining the main street at the turn. The gate was visible until then. Divaker turned back to wave his hand at Devyani. Uncle and Aunty waved back. Devyani was not there.